THE TINKER'S APPRENTICE

THE TINKER'S APPRENTICE

JORDAN CASTILLO PRICE

jCPBOOKS.com

Print edition published in the
United States in 2023 by JCP Books
www.jcpbooks.com

First Print Edition

ISBN-978-1-944779-35-1

Back when Sputnik first launched and Chubby Checker was doing the Twist, household items stopped rolling off the assembly line at Apex Magichanical Parts and Fittings, and their factory doors closed for good.

No one knows what happened to the Apex founders, and the blueprints have been lost to time. Fortunately, there are shops that specialize in repairing magichanical goods.

Shops like Arti-fix.

CONRAD

The smell of dubious bacon and overcooked egg tickled my senses as my hand hovered above the breakfast biscuits. They stood on the cart in an orderly row wrapped in wax paper, waiting to be snatched up by someone indiscriminate in taste and short on time.

And I'd been standing there so long, unable to decide, the crowd had changed over three times as annoyed commuters grabbed around me.

Ham. Sausage. Egg. Cheese. It wasn't as if there were all that many options.

And yet, I already knew that whichever sandwich I picked, I'd end up disappointed.

My friend Jeff had chosen our breakfast spot today–the food cart at the edge of Three Corners (*come on, Conrad, it's not so bad*)–and of course he'd picked the one cart where the sandwiches were either rubbery around the edges from the microwave or vaguely moist from a steam tray. Why? Because the cashier was a pretty girl with tattoos on her fingers and a violet streak in her hair...the type of girl who wouldn't in a million years give Jeff the time of day. In other words, the type of girl he couldn't resist.

Despite the fact that we've never once had a good sandwich from that particular cart, when Jeff had challenged me to pick somewhere else instead, I'd caved right in and agreed.

"Did you hear the latest rumor about the new building project on the edge of the city?" Jeff said. I hadn't, but of course he wasn't talking to me. Not with that flirtatious lilt. The girl with the finger tattoos answered with a bored shrug as she made change for her current customer. Unlike me, Jeff was undeterred by a show of disinterest, and he only took her non-answer as a challenge. "I hear a new Magimart is coming to town," he said dramatically.

That did pique the cool girl's interest. She deigned to raise a thin, penciled eyebrow. But I wasn't so sure how I felt about this new development. Sure, their selection was amazing and their prices were low, but... "If a Magimart opens up here, what will that mean for Three Corners?"

"What it always means," Jeff declared. "No more status quo. Survival of the fittest. All the mom-and-pop magic shops will either have to find a way to stay relevant...or close their doors."

Given that both Jeff and I worked for mom-and-pop magic shops, you'd think he wouldn't be quite so blasé about the whole thing. But I guess he didn't want to look fretful in front of his favorite cashier.

I settled on a sausage and cheese biscuit while Jeff speculated about all the wonderful things he'd heard you could buy at Magimart. Pens that wrote in any color, even ones you couldn't quite name. Electric toothbrushes people actually wanted to use. Candles that smelled like rainy mornings, or playing hooky, or days at the beach—and never burned down. "Affordable, too," he said. "So cheap that even Conrad could shop there."

I rolled my eyes, pulled out a crumpled five, and handed it to the girl. At least...I tried to. But before tattooed fingers could close around the bill, a scaly creature the size of a pineapple waddled out from behind a coffee urn and snatched it from my hand.

I winced. The cashier's auxiliar made me phenomenally uncomfortable—mainly because I could never quite tell exactly what it was supposed to be.

Auxiliars don't have a "true" form of their own. In terms of appearance, they ran the gamut from naturalistic animals to completely fantastic creatures. The way they appeared to human eyes all depended on the preference of their owners... and apparently this owner wanted an auxiliar that looked like a cross between a giant bat and a constipated pug. Jeff thought it was supposed to be a gargoyle, but every time I saw that squashed-in face, I couldn't help but think of the local dog park.

Unsettling as I might find the thing, I didn't want to be rude. I kept my face perfectly neutral as the gargoyle pug made change. The coins looked like Frisbees in its miniature human-like hands, but it counted them out quickly enough and handed them over. I made sure to angle my body so it couldn't see me wiping the coins on my pant leg before I pocketed my change.

I turned away from the food cart, doing my best not to wonder if the auxiliar was involved in making more than just change. Regardless of whether or not my food was prepared by its creepy little hands, I felt buyer's remorse the moment I peeled back the wax paper wrapper. The cheese had slid all to one side and congealed into the paper, while a big hunk of stale biscuit crumbled off and rolled down my jacket, only to be snatched up by an aggressive pigeon whose pinfeathers nearly took out my eye. The sausage, now exposed, gleamed grayly beneath a sheen of grease. It smelled like the bottom of an old Tupperware.

I'd forced down most of my bad sandwich by the time Jeff finally strode away from the food cart. Once we were out of earshot, he shot me a smug grin and whispered, "And you predicted she wouldn't say more than three words to me."

"*Are you gonna buy that?* doesn't count."

"It's only a matter of time before I wear her down."

I have no idea where Jeff gets his confidence. Not only is he pudgy and pale with incredibly thick glasses, but because he works at an ephemeral agents apothecary, odd smells tend to waft off him at inopportune times.

"Nothing ventured, nothing gained," Jeff went on. "When was the last time you strode up to someone and gave them your phone number?"

"How is this suddenly about me?"

"You should really capitalize on the fact that you dig sausage. I'd always thought it would be more straightforward if I was into that kind of thing. More insight into the thought process of the potential hook-up." Belatedly, I realized we were no longer talking about breakfast. "If I were you, I'd be out playing the field, hitting up guys left and right."

That was the thing, though. I didn't want "guys." I wanted someone special. It just so happened that I hadn't met that someone...yet.

We crossed the street and found ourselves approaching a jumble of small, colorful storefronts and oddball bits of statuary and signage affectionately known as Three Corners.

The Y-shaped intersection was one-third parking lot. But a hodgepodge of old businesses lined the stem of the Y, storefronts that smelled like dried flowers and old paper with the occasional whiff of vinegar and paraffin. Its businesses catered to very specific clientele: the sorts of folks willing to spend lots of time and energy on a magical hobby that was mercurial, at best. Simply put, old magic was expensive, and not everyone was willing to scrimp and save, sift and study, for the ability to change the color of an old pair of socks or predict where the closest parking spot might be. Not nowadays, when science and technology had much quicker solutions.

As we passed the Tome Repository, the vintage manuals in the window display beckoned seductively with their yellowed pages. But Jeff and I passed them every day, and we knew better than to get looped into reading a primer on magically inking your mimeograph machine. Any book you might pick up in Three Corners would be more of a curiosity than a tool. Entertaining, maybe. But not particularly relevant, not anymore. Not when you could just whip out your phone and Google anything you might need to know.

A page fluttered plaintively...or maybe I was just projecting. Because the Tome Repository had no way of making itself "relevant." And if Magimart really did set up shop in town, those books might as well be waving goodbye.

I was feeling nostalgic for the old neighborhood already, but Jeff was far more pragmatic. "It's time to update our résumés."

"What?" I stopped dead in my tracks in front of the auxiliar store. The repair shop where I worked, Arti-fix, was just across the street. Not that I was worried it could hear us. At least, I *hoped* it couldn't.

"Think about it, Conrad. You've been slaving away in that dusty old tinker shop for how long–months?" Actually, we were coming up on a year...but I could tell it wasn't to my advantage to point that out. "How many floors have you swept?"

"Just the one."

"And how many ephemeral agents have you restocked? How many shelves have you dusted? And how many sorry, thankless customers have you dealt with, day in, day out, with their broken doodads and ding dongs?"

"People get touchy when their magichanical stuff breaks down. It's not like you can just toss it out and buy a new one." Even as I said it, though, I had to wonder. Apex products were marvels of magical technology, back in the day. But even the ones we managed to repair still showed their age. There just wasn't as much call for a pipe-cleaner cleaner or a bouffant fluffer. Not like there was in 1955. But something new like a magichanical keyboard or cell phone case or GPS? People would go nuts for things like that, and not just the folks who liked magichanics for magic's sake. I eyed the Arti-fix storefront cautiously, wondering how it might be possible to stay relevant after all if enchanted household items started rolling off the assembly line again.

The store's prospects did not look good.

Jeff said, "Why the long face? It's not as if you actually enjoy working there."

"Hey, that's pretty harsh."

"Is it? I thought the whole reason you even applied was that you were hoping to get your hands dirty. Crack open some of those dusty old relics and see how they tick."

Not gonna lie. The mere thought of opening up an old Apex salad refresher, weightless bowling bag or silent radio had me itching to scuttle inside the shop and get to work. Unfortunately....

"Ol' Hester still hasn't let you touch anything," Jeff said, as if he could read my mind. "Nothing important, anyhow. Has she?"

I knew it was small of me to let Hester bear the blame for my lack of advancement, but it wasn't as if she'd care what Jeff thought of her. I just wasn't up for the razzing I'd get if he found out that in all this time, I wasn't able to begin my formal training because I hadn't picked out my primary tool.

CONRAD

I said goodbye to Jeff and let myself into the shop. By the soft light of the early morning, old Apex magichanicals roosted on their shelves like a flock of dozing metal chickens while dust motes danced in the air.

Arti-fix was so peaceful this time of day, without ringing phones and chatty customers, but you'd hardly call it quiet. Apex devices weren't technically alive...but they sure did have personalities. The contraptions in their varying stages of repair chatted like gossipy neighbors. The quiet clicking of gears on the spring-driven mechanics set a rhythm to the day like an industrial soundtrack. Interspersed with that cadence was an ambient hum from those items with electrical plugs...whether or not they were currently plugged into an outlet. And overlaying the texture of the clicking and humming were occasional oddball pops, pings and dings.

But another sound cut through the magichanical drone of the shop, a plodding thump I knew all too well. It was the sound of a bronze-tipped cane striking the floorboards.

With great annoyance.

The workroom door in back banged open and my boss strode through, squinting at me as if she maybe expected some random passer-by had discovered a key to the shop and let themselves in. Hester had been in business since Apex closed its doors, and the years hadn't been kind. Everything about her was grizzled and gray. Her fingers were crooked with arthritis, and she needed a cane to keep her balance. "It's about time," she snapped as I tossed my cheesy wax paper in the trash.

"Actually, I'm nearly five minutes early—"

Hester might be pushing eighty, but she's not particularly hard of hearing. Even so, she went on as if I hadn't said a word. "Young people nowadays have no work ethic. They think everything should just be handed to them. Back when I first got started, we didn't expect employers to keep us fed and entertained. There were no bring-your-dog-to-work days or incessant coffee breaks."

I was fairly sure that even way back then, people were allowed to at least eat, but I wasn't about to argue. I didn't want to get on Hester's bad side, considering what I'd been gearing up to ask. "Anyway, I'd been thinking, maybe it's time for me to start my training."

"Oh?" she said cautiously. "So you've finally settled on a tool?"

"Not...exactly."

Hester made a dismissive sound and turned toward her workroom door.

"But if you walk me through them one more time, I'm sure I can make my decision!"

There was no reason to think Hester would listen—she's

notoriously hard-headed—but just then, a rustle of feathers sounded from the workroom door. Hester's auxiliar: an iridescent, metallic peacock named Eureka.

Though it really should have been called *You-shriek-a* for the weird nonsense it babbled all day at the top of its lungs.

"Letmm!" the creature declared in an eerily human-sounding voice.

Hester paused and squinted down at the auxiliar. Even with its tail all tucked in, the creature was dazzling. Its metallic feathers sparkled so brightly, it threw dots of dancing light around the workroom like a walking disco-ball.

"Trytt," it added loudly.

Hester sighed. I'd steeled myself for her inevitable refusal when she shook her head in resignation and said, "Fine." She plucked a sheet of paper from her leather apron and slapped it down on the counter. "Finish everything on this list by the end of the day and I'll make time to acquaint you with your options. Again."

Hester was giving me a look sour enough to curdle milk, but who cared? I'd have a big epiphany today and finally make my decision—I could feel it!

"Don't cut any corners," she told me. "I'll be checking to make sure everything's up to my usual standards."

"Got it!" I snatched up the list, grinning eagerly. Hester narrowed her eyes. Eureka cocked its sparkly head. I grinned even wider and said, "You can count on me!"

With a harrumph, Hester turned around, clomped back into her workshop with her peacock auxiliar, and shut the door behind them with a very annoyed-sounding slam. The perpetual Do Not Disturb sign hanging on the doorknob rattled. I didn't worry myself about her annoyance, though.

I was too busy buzzing with adrenaline over the thought of finally embarking on my apprenticeship.

All I had to do was tackle Hester's to-do list.

STOCK PYRONETIC POWDER
SWEEP FLOOR
SHRED JUNK MAIL
EMPTY TRASH
WASH WINDOW

My heart sank. If not for that last item, I could plow through that list well before closing time. I emptied the trash every day. Swept the floor every other. Junk mail could be shredded between other tasks. And flyaway sparks from the pyronetic powder wouldn't cause me any trouble, provided I wore gloves. (You do *not* want to use the restroom with traces of pyronetic powder on your hands—ask me how I know.)

But the front window? The task would take an hour, at least. And that was if I was lucky enough to have zero customer interruptions. Hester's standards for the shop were nothing short of exacting—and customers were phenomenally demanding. All it would take was a single interruption, complete with a recounting of every possible detail about *how my Apex untoaster stopped working and now my bread is all crispy* to leave the window so streaky I'd need to start all over again.

I refused to let it come to that.

Working fast, I heaved the trash into the dumpster and tackled that floor quicker than an Apex Sweeps-a-Lot. I even got the pyronetic powder dispenser filled with only a minor singeing of my eyebrows. All the while, I did a mental pep-talk to gear up for tackling that plate glass window.

Just get started, I told myself, *and before you know it, the window will be gleaming like new. Won't Hester be thrilled when I tap on the workroom door and announce I've completed my list with time to spare? I'll bet she'll even smile. Not that she ever has before, not in my presence, at least...but there's a first time for everything! Quick, efficient, and thorough—that's me.*

I could feel it in my bones. Today was the day. Not only would I present Hester with a perfect, gleaming, squeaky-clean window, but I'd finally start learning about magichanical repair...for real!

Arti-fix is brimming with ephemeral agents, but we stock normal supplies, too. I filled a run-of-the-mill plastic bucket with entirely mundane water, splashed in some plain old regular ammonia, and approached the window with squeegee and brush.

The outside was covered in the sorts of things you'd imagine: water marks, chewing gum, general grime, and a few "gifts" from passing birds. But the inside would be the real challenge. It hadn't looked all that bad from the workbench, but once I got up close, I realized the glass was covered in an oily yellow haze. Ephemeral solvents and coatings—really, any magical aerosols—had a tendency to leave a particularly weird film behind.

But this film was no match for mundane ammonia.

I wet down a test patch and gave the cleaner a few seconds to do its thing. It bubbled up—a good sign. Enchanted residue can be phenomenally stubborn, but everyone knows bubbles mean something's working. The sticky yellow film became a *frothy* yellow film, and when I squeegeed off the test spot, it came clean with surprising ease.

Excited, I sudsed up the entire window. The dingy film started to froth. This was gonna be a breeze! And once the window was clean, I'd march right back to Hester's workroom and declare my readiness for a magichanical refresher.

I hoisted my squeegee and swept it across the glass. At first, all I saw was the sparkle of success. But then my focus shifted from the glass right in front of my face to the shop across the street—Helping Hands Auxiliars—and I noticed someone at their front window rolling up their blinds for the day.

Someone who was *way* more distracting than a demanding customer.

Of course it was rude to stare, but with the lights low and the sun angling against my window, I'd be effectively invisible. If the other guy even looked up, the only thing he'd see was his own reflection. And so I gawked shamelessly.

As the metal mesh rose, at first only his hips were visible. Slim, in low-slung jeans that hugged them in all the right places. Canted at an angle as if he held his weight on one leg, gracefully, like a model.

So as not to miss a thing, I quickly squeegeed the rest of the window as, inch by tantalizing inch, more of the mystery man was revealed. His T-shirt was nothing but a plain white undershirt—but on him, it was anything but boring. It clung in all the best places, and even treated me to a tiny flash of skin just below the hem as he reached up to straighten a few tangled slats.

The taper of his waist broadened into shoulders that filled out that clingy shirt just right. And as the hollow of his throat showed tan against the white fabric, I braced myself for the probability that once I saw his face, I'd have gotten myself all worked up for nothing.

...and soon realized that any caution I might have in that regard was entirely unfounded.

When I finally saw the man—all of him—I bonked my own forehead on the glass trying to get a better look.

He was striking, with dark hair tumbling over his forehead in a careless swoop. His face was all sharp, angular lines, with cheekbones for days. I'd never call him pretty. More like *interesting*...and that seemed infinitely more appealing.

Oddly enough, it wasn't his artfully tousled black hair, or his clingy T-shirt, or his painted-on jeans that grabbed my attention. Not that he was tall, and willowy, and remarkably graceful—though he was most definitely all these things and more. It was the ghost of a sultry smile that tugged at the corner of his mouth. Like he knew a secret...a really juicy one. And the thought of him turning that secret smile on me was enough to make me forget how to breathe.

I've always been a sucker for the mysterious type. Because, me? I'm exactly the opposite: the blond-haired, blue-eyed boy next door. The only reason anyone would cross the street when they saw me coming was if they were trying to avoid a hug.

I wondered if I could interest the hot guy at the auxiliar shop in a hug.

And I also wondered what it would take to get close enough to see the color of his eyes. The street was just wide enough that I couldn't quite tell whether they were light or dark, though maybe if I squinted just right....

He paused. Had his cryptic smile deepened, or was it just my imagination playing tricks on me? Had to be. He couldn't possibly see me, not at this time of morning when my lights were off and the sun was out. Which was a relief, since I'd just bonked my forehead again.

As I was trying to assess whether they were light or dark, those eyes flicked up and locked with mine.

I backpedaled, but thanks to a slick of sudsy ammonia water, traction was nil. As a result, I just danced in place, framed by my sparkling-clean window, flailing my dripping squeegee.

Talk about a first impression.

Hoping to make it seem like I'd totally meant to do that, I gave the squeegee another halfhearted wave. My heart nearly tripped over itself when the guy in the shop window raised his hand in return...but then, instead of waving back, he brushed a stray lock of hair off his forehead.

He hadn't seen me after all—he was just looking at his own reflection.

I was such an idiot...but at least I'd finished my window.

Before I could pat myself on the back, a customer barged in and said, "Excuse me!" More of a demand, honestly. She was a thirty-something woman, well put-together. There was a picture frame in her hand, and she brandished it like she meant business. A cute little boy of about four or five peeked out shyly from behind her. "This stopped working. I need it fixed."

Odd. Most Apex Magichanicals had moving parts, but Apexes we'd never seen before did crop up now and then. I directed the customer to the counter, pulled on a pair of white cotton gloves, and said, "May I?"

She handed it over, annoyed—with the magichanical, I told myself. Not me. Though she really was putting out a Karen vibe.

Hopefully I wouldn't give her anything to balk about.

I flicked on a work lamp and gave the frame a more thorough scrutiny. The miter at one of the corners was a bit loose, but overall the wood was in good condition. The glass was intact. I flipped it face-down and took note of the little sawtoothed grip up at the top, with the words Self-Leveling Technology printed just above it. Aha. That's where the magic would be.

The maker's mark stamped into the metal was faint and somewhat tarnished, but even so, something about it seemed "off." I adjusted my lamp and took a better look through my magnifying glass.

At first glance, it looked like an Apex brand-mark. But on closer inspection, the stylized mountain was just a bit too sharp. And instead of *Apex*, the nearly indiscernible lettering beneath read *Pinnacle*.

In other words, a knock-off.

"I'm so sorry," I told the customer, "but this isn't a magichanical."

"But it's a self-leveling picture frame. What else could it be?"

"Apex was the only company that used genuine magichanical parts on their assembly line. Other manufacturers tried to imitate their products by adding some ephemeral agents, but eventually they can run dry—"

"I paid a lot of money for this. Nearly double what a normal frame would run me."

And if it were a true Apex, she would have paid significantly more...but I've learned the hard way that customers who already feel cheated don't care that their knock-off was a bargain. "I'm sorry," I said again—not that the apologies seemed to be getting me anywhere. "We can only repair genuine Apex products."

The customer's eyes went steely, and I clenched in all my most private places, knowing beyond the shadow of a doubt that the next words out of her mouth would be, *Let me speak to your manager*—until we were interrupted by a loud, wet *blat*. Followed by a giggle.

The little boy had parked himself in front of my sparkling clean window, shoved his moist little face up against the glass, and blown.

Blat!

At his age, I would have thought this was the height of comedy. Heck, even now, I bet it looked pretty darned funny from the other side of the window—even though the whole thing was now covered in spitty little face-prints. But as the owner of the non-Apex picture frame reveled in her entitlement and lambasted me with a long string of insults, all the humor drained from the situation. I was left with only the realization that I'd need to start the window all over again... and the disappointment that I was unlikely to pick out my first tool anytime soon.

3

RUNE

My glance out the front window was informative—waking up usually does involve a bit of catch-up. This time around, had I been asleep for five hours, five years...or five decades? I could've sworn I'd felt a good bit of time whizzing by, but you never know.

Evidently, cars were still in use, and they looked similar to what I remembered...more or less. The glorious chrome grilles and impressive swooping fins were gone, but they weren't flying, and they still had a hood, four tires and a steering wheel. The clothing wasn't all that different, either. And the shop had hardly changed a bit. I was musing on this fact when I was distracted by a familiar tut of displeasure.

A bony black cat was perched on top of a nearby bannister, regarding me through narrowed eyes—one yellow, one pale blue. What a relief to see a friendly face—okay, maybe *friendly* was a stretch. But a face I'd certainly grown accustomed to over the aeons. "Helix! If you're still around, then everything's jim-dandy!"

"Honestly, Rune." She rolled her eyes. "People don't say

that anymore."

"No?" I glanced out the window. "But I see they still wear dungarees."

"And they don't say that, either."

"I'd been hoping pantaloons might come back in style. It's so fun to say—*pantaloons*. And they really brought out my calves."

Ignoring me, Helix stood and gave a stretch, arching her back impossibly high. Her tail curled crookedly. She folded back into a sitting position and wrapped it primly around her paws. "I was starting to think you'd never wake up. I must've knocked you off that shelf a hundred times."

"Why bother? If you're feeling social, there are plenty of others around to help you pass the time. I can feel them."

The bent tip of Helix's tail gave a single twitch. "I'm not feeling *lonely*, you ninny. I've got news."

Languor still had its teeth in me, the feeling that I could nod off at any moment and wake up again decades later to everyone prancing around in delightfully modern pantaloons...but at the sound of news, I felt myself perk up. Helix regarded melodrama with great disdain. If she found something newsworthy, no doubt it *must* be juicy.

"I'm all ears," I said. "They still say *that*, don't they?"

Helix's tail twitched again. "Anyway. I overheard our landlord wringing his hands with his friend on the Chamber of Commerce—"

"Overheard," I murmured, smiling.

"Well, they carry their telephones everywhere nowadays and start spouting off wherever the mood takes them—is it my fault he had this conversation right under my nose?"

"I can't wait to see this."

"Believe me, it's nothing to write home about. Apparently, there's a rumor that the smaller shops may go out of business. There's a new game in town and they simply can't compete."

I threw up my hands. "But I only just settled in."

"It's been nearly seventy-five years."

"And now I'm expected to move again? No, this just won't do."

Helix gave a feline shrug. "If this is where you want to stay, it's not as if anyone can stop you. But you never know what will become of this shop. It may become a fast food place."

"*Fast* food? You're expected to catch it now?"

My friend ignored the question. She was on a roll. "The shop could be turned into condominiums. Or it might just be razed to the ground. My point is, you've been alone for far too long already. How will you click with a decent counterpart if there's nothing here but a pile of rubble?"

She did have a point. Long ago, before "fast food", before pantaloons, humankind was more like us, and it was easy to find common interests. To mingle. To bond. But nowadays it felt as if we were speaking two different languages...modern slang notwithstanding. This shop had set itself up as the type of place where one of us might find a good counterpart, and the humans who came searching were predisposed to have the right sort of mindset.

And even then, no one had managed to rouse me.

Others must have found their counterparts, though. The shelves around me were all empty, all but the tattered velveteen cushion, faded with age, that bore the imprint of Helix's bony rump and a liberal coating of black fur.

"They're all in the showroom," she said when she saw me

taking in the empty spaces. "They picked up on the rumor that the shop won't be around forever. They're so worried it will close up and leave us all out on the street, they're scrambling to outdo each other, hoping to attract a good match. Or, frankly, any match at all. Suddenly everyone's casting themselves as a puppy or a kitten or a fuzzy little hatchling. Pandering to the lowest common denominator."

"But not you."

"Of course not." She licked a paw and smoothed her whiskers. "When my counterpart sees me, they will simply know we are meant to be together. No amount of superficial cuteness will change that."

Maybe not. But looks certainly never hurt.

The layout of the shop was the same as I remembered, with its carved woodwork, deep shelves and stamped tin ceilings. The carpet was new and the light fixtures were different—which meant both carpeting and electricity were still in vogue. I followed the rise and fall of voices, keeping to the shadows. Pausing in the recess of the tall shelving, I peered into the main showroom, not wanting to let on how difficult it was to even walk when it had been so long since I'd bothered to stretch my legs.

It turned out my caution was unwarranted. The others were putting on such a show, no one would have noticed me at all unless I was crashing together a set of cymbals and trumpeting a song on a giant kazoo.

Did they still make kazoos?

"You weren't kidding," I told Helix, who slunk back and forth through my ankles. "The others are really hamming it up for that woman."

The customer in search of an auxiliar was young and very

thin, in extremely tight dungarees—or whatever it was they were called nowadays. The denim slacks were dark blue, as if they were brand new and fresh from the indigo dye, and yet a trio of frayed holes graced one thigh, so perfectly spaced it was almost as if they'd been deliberately cut.

How strange.

Her loosely curled hair was quite long, her makeup exaggerated, and her handbag tiny. Several auxiliars scampered around at her feet, yipping and tumbling and enthusiastically wagging their adorable little tails. "You're sure they won't get too much bigger?" the customer asked.

I noticed the clerk she was speaking with. Somehow the clerks always felt the same, a bland, benign presence. This one seemed decent enough—a middle-aged man with a shiny bald head and a ready smile...but entirely lacking in that elusive "something" that made certain humans so intriguing.

"You want a *small* auxiliar?" he asked, as though he thought he must surely have misunderstood the young woman. "Size is no issue. They can be as big or small as you need them to be."

"So long as they fit in my purse." She bent at the waist, made kissy faces at the "puppies" and added in baby-talk, "Isn't that right? Isn't it??"

The clerk tried a different tack. "Bonding with your auxiliar isn't the same as getting a pet—they'd know better than to wander off."

True. And if they ever got sick of that squeaky little baby-talk voice, no mere handbag would keep them from slipping away, hunkering down somewhere safe, and settling in for a nice long nap.

I was unsure if the hopefuls were keyed up on the challenge

of competing with one another, or if they were truly smitten with the girl in the artfully ripped dungarees. While the humans looked elsewhere, even between blinks, the auxiliars pulled themselves in tight, like an obese man at the beach hoping to impress a girl in a bikini. Were bikinis still in style? At any rate, the ones who'd become invested in fitting themselves inside a handbag grew smaller, and cuter, and cuddlier. Their eyes grew bigger and wider-set, and their tiny yips and barks pitched higher. They wagged and wriggled, pranced and preened.

So much work. I was exhausted just looking at them.

The heart wants what it wants, though, and if they felt a potential connection, I could hardly blame them for trying.

A palpable wave of longing rose from the group. It almost made me want to ball myself up into a furry little package and go scampering off toward the young woman myself.

"Don't tell me you're actually considering it," Helix said.

I thought about how much effort it would take to figure out a new form, one I wasn't particularly familiar with, at that. Chances of me carrying it off—and being "cuter" than the others, to boot—were slim, at best. Even so... "What if I *am* tempted? Maybe I'm bored with being alone."

"And what difference does it make when you're always asleep?"

I ignored the jibe and watched the others to scope out my competition. They weren't just cute, they were memorable. Some with floppy ears, others perky. Some with sleek, velvety coats, others huge puffballs of fur. Their colors ranged from light to dark, even pastel tones you'd never find in nature. Surely one of them would be the auxiliar of the young woman's dreams.

Sometimes, though, having too many options is daunting. The customer overloaded on cuteness and told the clerk she'd "think about it." But as she turned to go, a pathetic yip cut through the chaos, followed by a thin, heartbreaking whine. "Oh no!" the woman in the dungarees said. "It's hurt its wittle paw!"

At her feet, the auxiliar limped theatrically a few steps, then locked eyes with her and treated her to a shy wag of the tail.

Wow. He was good.

"This one," the customer said, snuggling the auxiliar to her chest and planting kisses on his fuzzy head.

"You're sure?" the clerk said, baffled by the customer's sudden change of heart. "Our refund policy is very strict."

"This one," she repeated firmly. And within moments, grinning a canine grin, the lucky bastard rode out of the store with his head poking out the top of the young woman's handbag.

"Now you see what we're up against," Helix said. "Suddenly everyone's turning somersaults in hopes of snatching up the next counterpart."

Which wouldn't matter...if she truly believed what she'd said about holding out for the perfect one. I reached down and stroked her behind the ears. She pretended not to care, but I saw her furry back ripple in response. "If all else fails," I told her, "we can always settle in for a little snooze and rouse ourselves when the competition's not quite so fierce. Let's put an egg in our shoe and beat it."

Helix snapped to her feet and shook off my hand. "That's it—I can't take any more of your appalling slang. I need to get you up to date. Right now."

I followed as she slunk past the shelves, leading me into a back office. Like the showroom, it hadn't changed much. Same plaster walls, same hardwood floors, same windows and doors. The furniture was new—simpler shapes and cleaner lines, arranged in a different configuration—but an office was still an office, and the stacks of unfiled paperwork weren't much different from piles I'd seen before.

Helix hopped up onto the desk, stepping with great precision to avoid causing a paper avalanche. She tapped a small plasticky briefcase with one paw. "Open this."

I did as she asked, and found a typewriter inside. The inside of the lid lit up. "Where are the actual typing bits? And what are all those little colored pictures?"

"There are no typing bits. It's called a laptop computer, and those icons on the screen are files."

I turned the device this way and that. "What magichanical parts make up the action?"

"None. It's completely mundane."

"But where does the paper feed in?"

"It's in the printer across the room."

"So now you need *two* different devices to type something out? Technology's taken a step backward, if you ask me."

Helix swatted my hand. "Forget about *typing* for half a second and tap that little red icon."

I poked at it, and the image changed. "It's like a television set!"

"More or less. This is called YouTube. And I can't think of a better way to get you all caught up on the current state of affairs than to subject you to a few hours of random videos."

While it didn't hold any paper, maybe the "laptop computer" was more useful than I'd originally thought. Though after a few hours, once I'd acquainted myself with clothes and hairstyles and advertisements and slang, things started to blend together.

Despite my best efforts, I felt my eyelids grow heavy.

Maybe Helix was right and the shop's days were numbered. But after several dozen videos, I decided I was simply too exhausted to watch even one more viral kitchen hack. Surely no one would begrudge me a short nap....

4

CONRAD

To say I didn't finish Hester's to-do list was the understatement of the year. By the time I was ready to lock up Arti-fix for the night, the trash was overflowing again, the floors were dusted with various bits of crud, and more greasy prints had appeared on my newly cleaned window. So I was beyond surprised when, despite my inability to hold up my end of the bargain, Hester thumped out of her workroom and heaved a stout metal toolbox onto the counter with a sharp clang.

She snapped open the toolbox. On one side was a compliment of mundane tools—the usual suspects, like screwdrivers, wrenches, hammers and files. But on the other were the fantastical things you can't get in a hardware store—the tools made by Apex itself. These tools held the place of honor, each nestled in its own plush-lined compartment. They ticked and chittered amongst themselves as if commenting on a mildly interesting golf match.

The tools themselves had the sleek, curved, midcentury look of all Apex products, each one made to fit in the hand just so. Some were electric, some powered by magical agents, and others ran on good, old-fashioned elbow grease. One thing they all had in common was that they were incredibly powerful...and, in the wrong hands, even somewhat dangerous.

"Here's the spiel," she said. "You've heard it from me before—and you'll keep on hearing it until it finally sinks in. A journey of a thousand miles begins with a single step, and the first step toward magichanical repair mastery is the selection of your primary tool."

I swallowed hard.

"Only once you've gained complete proficiency in a tool can you even think about adding another to your arsenal. I've mastered six tools over the course of my career, and I started early. No monkeying around with half-finished liberal arts degrees and gap years. Just as soon as I was old enough to take up a trade, I apprenticed the local tinker."

She pulled a single tool from its velvet compartment, something that looked like a cross between a mechanical claw and an eggbeater. "The Spintastic," she said. "Its workings are so convoluted, it was nearly a month before I could so much as turn it on without finding myself wandering down the block backwards. Ended up lost more times than I could count—the neighbors got used to sitting me down till my head stopped spinning then sending me off to the workshop again. You can't imagine how satisfying it is to finally crack a tough nut like this after years of trying."

I swallowed again.

"But once I finally did..." Hester gazed at the tool with an appreciative sigh. "Even the most stubborn threaded fastener was no match for me. So. Once you decide which tool to start with, we'll begin."

And there was the crux of my problem. Choosing my starting point.

Decisions hadn't always been my Achilles' heel. In fact, when I was a kid, I was forever badgering my mom to let me pick out my own clothes. Sixth grade, she finally relented—and I strutted into junior high in the purplest winter coat you ever saw.

Only to be known as Conrad the Concord Grape for the rest of the year.

Luckily, we moved that summer and I ended up in a different school. And mom picked out a new parka for me the next winter, even though the purple one still technically fit. But I still can't look a grape in the eye without shuddering.

My first tool would have far greater ramifications than a winter coat, since my mom couldn't grab me a new one at JC Penney. I'd be stuck with my choice for years. Maybe even decades. Heck, for all I knew, even if Hester managed to keep the shop open in the face of Magimart, she wouldn't even live long enough to finish training me in a single tool. Overwhelm hit hard, and I found myself wondering if maybe I should have pursued that degree in nontraditional puppeteering after all, and exactly how many credits I might need to complete it.

How could I possibly choose when the ramifications were so sweeping?

Hester peered at me over the side of the open toolbox. "Conrad? What's gotten into you? You're as white as a sheet."

As I searched for an excuse that wouldn't leave me looking like a complete flake, I spotted Eureka judging me from the workroom with the harsh gaze of its baleful metallic eye. "Nreedy!" it shrieked.

An awkward pause...and then Hester tucked her Spintastic away. She dusted her hands together and said, "We'll leave this be for the moment. I haven't got time for any of your hemming and hawing just now. It's late, and I'm no spring chicken."

If she considered my momentary lapse into silence to be "hemming and hawing," I'd hate for her to see me weigh the pros and cons of such a monumental decision aloud. Thankfully, she put away her toolbox, and followed by her disconcerting auxiliar, headed home without another word.

Once I locked up the shop for the night, I found Jeff waiting for me on the sidewalk outside, looking pointedly at his watch. I wasn't paying much attention to him, though. Across the street at Helping Hands Auxiliars, the blinds were rolling down.

After my conversation with Hester, I'd been totally baffled by the thought of picking out a tool. But a glimpse at that window reminded me of the new clerk I'd glimpsed opening up the shop, and my overwhelm gave way to excitement. No tough decisions here—that man was someone I wanted to know better for sure! Once I elbowed Jeff out of my way, I finally got a look at the person lowering the blinds...but it wasn't my guy from earlier that morning. Just the same cheerful bald man I normally saw opening and closing the store.

When Jeff saw me staring at the storefront, he said, "Since when were you in the market for a helper-monkey?"

I...wasn't. Not until he asked that question, anyhow, and I thought about the way Eureka seemed to have an opinion about the things Hester did...an opinion Hester apparently valued. If I had a companion like that—something devoted only to me, to help me work through the pros and cons of a decision—I wouldn't get so tripped up every time I needed to make a choice. "Maybe it's time I finally took the leap and invested in an auxiliar."

"But I saw the way you looked at the gargoyle on the food cart this morning. You could barely touch your change."

True. The mere thought of that squashed-in little face made me shudder.

At home that night in my apartment, sitting at my hand-me-down dining room table over a can of forgettable soup, I turned over the idea of actually shopping at Helping Hands. Obviously, I'd never adopt a scary auxiliar. Not on purpose. But they're capable of changing shape, or so I'm told—though as far as I can tell, Hester's screaming peacock has never been anything but a judgy, slightly terrifying metallic bird.

How many times had I gone shopping, only to be underwhelmed by my purchase the moment I got home? Too many times to count. Choosing a lousy sandwich was one thing. The worst you'd end up with was a little heartburn, and even that would fade by lunchtime. Auxiliars were forever.

I couldn't pick out a tool. Heck, I couldn't even pick out a food cart. How could I ever settle on an auxiliar?

Then again, maybe this could all work to my advantage. Choosing an auxiliar—a permanent decision—was something no one would expect to be taken lightly.

One might even return to the store several times...at several different points in the day...to ponder one's decision.

In other words, it couldn't hurt to shop.

Especially when shopping meant seeing more of the guy in the clingy white T-shirt.

By the time I climbed into bed, I considered the matter settled. Until the doubts began to creep in.

What if, in the process of visiting the shop, I truly did find my heart set on a particular auxiliar? They were so expensive, I'd never even been tempted to window shop. Not on my current paycheck. But now that I'd finally talked myself into visiting the store, I simply couldn't let the idea go.

I rolled over and checked my clock. Nearly eleven.

But it wasn't eleven o'clock in Hawaii. In fact, it wasn't even late.

It took a few tries—connections are really dicey at sea— but eventually, I did get through. My mother's face filled the video chat looking extremely concerned and way too tan. "Conrad? Can you hear me?"

"I can hear you just fine."

"There's so much glare off the water I can hardly tell it's you." She shielded her eyes with her free hand and called out to my father, "George, your son is calling." Several minutes ensued of her wandering around, trying to find the spot with the best connection and the least glare. When she finally settled in, she asked, "Is everything okay? You look tired."

My father joined her. Also looking very tan. "It's the middle of the night on the mainland."

"Uh, not exactly," I said. "And I'm fine. Everyone's fine. I was just hoping—"

"Wait, there's a lag," Mom said, and the image of the two of them pixelated, rearranged itself, and continued on...

though with the voice not quite matching the video. "Did you read those links I sent you about vitamin D? Another study just came out."

"I feel fine," I said quickly, hoping to slot into the conversation despite the weird lag. "Listen, the reason I called was that I want to buy an auxiliar."

Mom frowned hard while Dad looked puzzled, and I began to wonder if I was barking up the wrong tree with them. "You've always told me that if I really, truly wanted something, there was a nest egg you could tap into and help me out. Well, now's the time. I want to take the next step in my magichanical career. I want an auxiliar."

Okay, technically I just wanted to look. But if I really fell for a particular auxiliar, only to have it snatched out from under my nose because I couldn't cough up the cash, I'd never forgive myself. I'd had that happen too many times with potential boyfriends—guys who ended up being swept off their feet by someone more decisive when I second-guessed myself about letting them know how I felt. I wasn't about to let it happen with an auxiliar.

My parents' image went blocky for a moment, then cleared. "Say that again," Mom yelled over the wind. "I thought you said you wanted an auxiliar."

"Yes! That's exactly what I said."

Now Dad frowned hard and Mom looked puzzled...and it wasn't just a fleeting twitch of the eyebrows captured by a frozen screen. Dad said, "Wouldn't you rather go back to school? I'm sure you could finish one of your degrees in just a semester or two!"

"Why finish something I wasn't interested in to begin with?"

"How about a boat?" my mother yelled, clasping her sun-hat to her head to keep it from flying into the surf. "You'd love a boat—they're so much fun!"

"You know I get seasick."

Dad said, "An RV, then. Think of all the cool places you could see in an RV."

"Listen to me," I pleaded. "You guys are big on pursuing your dreams. Well, I have a dream, too—and it's *my* dream. I don't want to sail or puppeteer or drive around looking for campsites. I want to pursue magichanicals. I want an auxiliar."

"Is this about the clock?" Mom said.

I glanced up at the stately piece hanging on my bedroom wall—the only decor in the room. If I could get it working again, it would be more than just a mere conversation piece. But even if I didn't, it was still a valuable piece of magichanical history.

It was a good-sized wall clock, nearly two feet wide at the broadest point and half again as tall. The design looked simple, but only at first glance. A closer look revealed that it was all curves, not a square angle anywhere on it. The detailing was all simple—from the subtly domed glass covering the face to the gilded hours—but so beautifully proportioned and masterfully crafted, it veritably screamed craftsmanship and quality.

Unfortunately, that craftsmanship was currently on the fritz.

Dad said, "We know you love that thing as much as your grandfather did. But fixing it won't bring him back."

"I know," I said. But I did think he'd be smiling down at me if I made it happen.

Mom said, "Just what is it you think an auxiliar will do for you?"

"It's no secret how much I hate making decisions—"

"Not another purple coat situation," Dad groaned.

I forged ahead. "I just think a partner I can really trust—a sentient, magical partner, one who can look at things from a fresh perspective and help me see what's going on—will totally turn things around. No more settling for whatever randomly happens while I'm waffling on a decision. An auxiliar will help me get on the right track and straighten out my life."

For people who gave up everything to live on a boat, my parents didn't seem very keen on me following my bliss—though they did eventually decide that while they thought I'd be much happier with a drum kit or a dune buggy, if what I truly wanted was an auxiliar, they'd be willing to help me out.

The next morning, I bought not one terrible sandwich from the food cart, but two. By lunchtime, the second one was practically fossilized, but I was able to skip buying lunch and scarf it down on my way across the street...mostly. The last bite turned out to be particularly stubborn.

I stood there on the sidewalk outside Helping Hands in my best sweater—I'm told it brings out the blue in my eyes—and repeatedly attempted to swallow the congealed wad of microwaved biscuit that was lodged somewhere in my esophagus. As I did, I noticed I was in a prime spot to see between two high wooden shelves into a sort of alcove at the end of the aisle. And in that alcove was the guy who'd nearly made me trip over my own squeegee.

He sat on the floor with his back against the wall and his

knees pulled up, with a pattern of sunlight-through-window-pane angling across his body. There was a black cat beside him. It looked like they were looking at a phone...together.

My first thought was that it was one of those interactive apps with animated fish to keep a cat entertained (or to keep an owner entertained while the cat smacked the screen in frustration.) But then the guy said something, murmuring quietly as he smiled his secret smile. The cat touched the screen with a very un-cat-like gesture and I realized it wasn't a cat at all. It was his auxiliar.

I swallowed hard. The sandwich wad mercifully cleared my esophagus, and I let myself into the cozy dimness of the shop.

Helping Hands was the same sort of antique storefront as Arti-fix, with old woodwork, high ceilings, and an ever-present scattering of dust floating in the shafts of light that eked through the warren of shelving. But where my shop was still and quiet, save for the clicks, ticks and hums of the Apex Magichanicals, this place had energy.

I hadn't realized the auxiliars would be talking. Weird.

Squawks and yips, chortles and chitters. The sounds filled the space with a background wall of companionable chatter like a busy neighborhood coffee shop. It was surprisingly comforting...but unexpectedly disorienting. While Arti-fix had a simple layout designed to get customers to the register in a single straight shot, the auxiliar shop was more of a maze. Try as I might to trace a path to the clerk I'd just seen through the window, I found nothing but empty aisles and dead ends.

It was when I shifted my perception to navigate with my ears instead of my eyes that I finally made some headway.

At first, it was just a few empty cages and the odd scattering of feathers or fur on some otherwise bare shelves. But as I followed the sound of the conversation, the shelves got more lived-in. Toys and treats, cushions and tanks.

Soon, I turned the corner and the shelving opened into a room where a tumble of puppies played on the floor under the watchful eyes of a sales clerk. Not the clerk with the secret smile, I noted with no little disappointment, but the friendly-looking fellow with the shiny bald head.

His eyes brightened when he saw me. "Ah, a customer!" he announced to the room at large, and the sound of the animal chattering quieted as if someone had turned down the volume knob until it was more of a background ambiance. "And what can I help you find today?"

The sales clerk with the amazing cheekbones.

Of course I didn't say so. That would be rude. But I did try to sneak a surreptitious glance around whenever he looked away. Auxiliars were everywhere: the shelves, the counter, and even the floor. Surely they'd have enough sense not to be stepped on, since they're supposed to be incredibly smart. But I had to shuffle in carefully so as not to step on the puppy pile tumbling around my feet.

"I didn't realize they'd be so young," I said.

"Oh?" said the clerk.

He was still smiling, but the way he'd said it made me think I might be missing something. And what did I really know about the life cycle of an auxiliar? I'd always thought of them like a phoenix that went in and out of hibernation, emerging into each new incarnation as a fully-formed adult. But I supposed new auxiliars had to come from somewhere. One of them must have had a litter. Or a gaggle. Or maybe a brood. Or...whatever a batch of little baby auxiliars might be called.

"See anyone you like?" the clerk asked.

One fluffy puppy was tugging at my shoelace and another had rolled onto its back, wriggling adorably, while a third sat up on its hind legs, grinning. But.... "I was looking for something a little less...canine?"

Thankfully, the clerk didn't think I was a monster for not wanting a puppy. "Of course. The form an auxiliar takes is never set in stone, but like you and me, they do have their own personalities and preferences."

As he spoke, I found myself staring at a small roundish object on the credenza behind him. Softly colored. Greenish, or gray-ish, with a subtle undertone of blue. At first I took it for a lump of polished gemstone, but the surface didn't look entirely hard. Some sort of exotic succulent—a spineless cactus, perhaps. But there was no pot, no soil. A fossil, then? Or maybe an urchin.

"How about a cat?" the clerk suggested, bringing me back to the matter at hand.

I supposed it couldn't hurt to look at them, though ever since my aunt's beloved cat threw up in my best shoes, I wasn't a big fan. But an auxiliar wouldn't do anything like that (hopefully). And besides, if I owned a feline auxiliar, I'd have something in common with the guy with the cheekbones. It would even give me a good excuse to come back after I bought the cat, looking for advice.

"Okay," I said. "Show me the cats."

The man gestured toward my feet. "They're right there."

Sure enough, the furballs I'd taken for puppies weren't pup-pies at all, but fluffy little kittens, and the yips and yaps were actually meows and mews.

"Go ahead," the man said with an encouraging smile. "Pick

one up. Get a feel for it."

I'd never purposely touched an auxiliar before. You hear a lot of love-at-first-sight stories, so maybe my expectations were too high. Not that I expected fireworks, necessarily. But at least some kind of spark.

Unfortunately, when I picked up one of the wiggling, chirruping balls of fluff, I felt nothing but a queasy nervousness that I'd somehow manage to offend the magical creature in my grasp.

"You're doing great," the bald man said. "Try talking to it."

The only thing running through my head was *omigod-omigod-omigod*, which hardly made for scintillating conversation. Why did I ever think this was a good idea? I felt like such an idiot.

"You could introduce yourself," the man suggested kindly.

"Uh...hello. I'm Conrad." The kitten stared up at me with luminous eyes, no doubt hoping it didn't have to go home with a total goofus like me. "Nice to meet you," I said awkwardly, and then reached out with my fingertips for a handshake. I was relieved to see it understood me as it extended its little paw...only to discover its claws were sharper than needles.

"Yeeowch!" I cried, and for a split second, the auxiliar was airborne—until its tail whipped out and wrapped three times around my wrist.

I may not know much about cats...but I was fairly certain their tails didn't do that. When I tried to shake my hand free, those needle-like claws found purchase in my sweater... and my chest beneath it. I jumped. The kitten clung hard, bleating out a sound somewhere between a startled meow and a smoke detector.

Stiff-armed and panicked, I somehow detached the demon in a kitten body from my torso and thrust it back into the hands of the befuddled clerk—though several spots on my sweater unraveled and went right along with it. Blue yarn stretched taut between us for a moment like entrails...then dropped down against my belly as the "kitten" retracted its claws and let out a tiny, adorable *mew*.

5

RUNE

"Wake up, already! You missed all the action!" Helix's words woke me just as she swatted me in the rump and sent me sprawling on the floor.

I began to doubt the wisdom of telling her to alert me if anything scandalous was going on.

The room was filled with hopefuls, all of them arguing amongst themselves, second-guessing and finger-pointing. Or claw-pointing, as the case may be, as most of them were shaped like kittens...more or less.

"Amateurs," Helix grumbled.

We each have a handful of forms we've perfected over the years. But in a pinch, we can shift into whatever we can imagine. *Holding* that shape successfully is a different story.

"—and now you've ruined it for all of us!" a white fluffball of a kitten snarled in a low, gravelly voice.

The whole mob of feline auxiliars was centered on a Siamese kitten struggling to extricate its claws from a wad of blue yarn. No matter which way it pulled, it only seemed to tangle itself further. With a huff of frustration, it shifted, ballooning suddenly into a fully-grown opossum with a shaggy, dun-colored coat, black bead-like eyes, and a mobile, hairless pink tail. With now-powerful jaws, it snapped the yarn from its claws and spat it to one side. "It's not my fault the kid was such a sissy," he said. "If he can't handle a little scratch, he has no business shopping for a kitten."

"The claws are retractable," a tiger-striped kitten said with a long-suffering sigh—though she was walking on her hind legs as she said it. She paused by the front window, scanned the sidewalk outside, and said, "He's not coming back."

Tension went out of the room as the auxiliars released their unaccustomed forms, and the litter of kittens blossomed into a menagerie of different creatures—mammals, reptiles, and everything in between. Not only was there a boar and a faun and a Komodo dragon. A furry alligator with antlers slunk away toward the shadowy recesses of the shop. A goat shook out its tiny silver wings. And a moth with the face of a fox fluttered up toward the ceiling to butt itself against the overhead light.

The floorboards groaned as the white fluffball morphed into a rhinoceros with a tuft of white hair on its warty gray head. He said, "The shop is on its way out—and people don't partner with auxiliars nearly as often as they used to. We can't be driving off our potential humans. If you don't know how to be a damn kitten, step aside and let the rest of us take our best shot."

A six-legged meerkat popped up from behind the counter. "Don't be such an alarmist. We don't know for sure the shop will close."

A platypus harrumphed and narrowed its tiny eyes.

"You're just saying that so you can swoop in on the next counterpart."

The rhino shifted nervously. "The shop will close and we'll be out on the streets. Fine for now, but mark my words— come winter, we'll all be sorry. Not to mention all that traffic. How many of us will end up as roadkill?"

"You're certainly in no danger of being flattened by a car," Helix said brusquely. "Instead of wringing our hands, we need a contingency plan, simple as that."

"Like what?" the platypus demanded.

Helix gave a convincingly feline shrug. "We could all be people."

That idea caused a big stir, to put it mildly.

Once all the honking, snarling and bleating subsided, she added, "Just look at Rune. He's a person right now—and no one ever questions whether or not he really is one. How hard can it be?"

"It must be exhausting," the fox-moth called down from the ceiling. "Rune spends most of his time asleep."

And that was all I heard before I curled up against the shelves and felt my eyelids flutter closed.

CONRAD

Luckily, there were no customers milling around outside Arti-fix when I fled the auxiliar store clutching the shreds of my dignity—and my favorite sweater. I thought I was home free to just nip across the street...so, naturally, Jeff picked that moment to step outside the apothecary and grab the mail.

"What on earth happened to you?" he called over.

"Nothing."

"Were you looking at auxiliars?"

"None of your business."

"You actually touched one of them?"

"No comment!"

"And isn't that your favorite sweater?"

I pulled out my key, hoping to slip into Arti-fix and away from the embarrassing interrogation, but Jeff's scrutiny had me all flustered, and I fumbled with the lock.

Jeff craned his neck and looked me up and down. "What on earth were you trying to cuddle, a scissor-handed sloth?"

"Never mind."

"Well, that tired old sweater was getting a little stretched out, anyhow. Now you've got a good excuse to buy a new one."

Favorite things weren't exactly replaceable. But I wasn't about to stand out there and debate the fact with Jeff with a giant hole in my top.

I slipped inside none too soon and flipped over the "be back soon" sign hanging on the door so the "open" side was facing the street. The shop was quiet, save for its usual tick-tocks and hums, and I was alone. What a relief. I let out a breath I didn't know I'd been holding and turned my sweater around so the hole was in the back. True, the neckline rode up and pinched at my Adam's apple...but at least customers wouldn't see the shredded mess if I kept facing front.

As I went about my to-do list, I was overly aware of the hole, positive a customer would burst in at the worst possible moment and behold my sweater in all its hole-riddled glory. But as I ticked off task after task, eventually I fell into a zone where I stopped worrying about humiliating myself in front of customers and focused on finishing off that list.

Dusting the bookshelf was the last item on my list—a task that was nowhere near as fun since we sold the refurbished Apex Dust-o-Rama—but I supposed a mini-vacuum would do the trick. Being up close and personal with the shelves made me realize I hadn't really gone through the contents since I first started working there.

I discovered an old manual with yellowed pages and a cracked cover, and ran my thumb down the softened edges of the pulpy pages. Back in the day, magichanical tools came by mail-order. Nowadays, you had to hope for something to crop up in an online auction. But Hester owned a few spares she could pass along to a worthy apprentice, and at some point, she'd helpfully bookmarked those pages.

Shopping for a tool via catalog seemed a lot less intimidating than handling the real things. Maybe I could actually do this, with or without an auxiliar's help! I flipped to the first sticky note and dove in with the intention of choosing my starting tool once and for all.

The Spintastic was out. The world was dizzying enough without adding gyroscopic confusion to the mix. I passed that by and paged over to the next bookmark.

The Rejoinder was a powerful tool that could bond things together without the need of adhesive. It was a tong-shaped apparatus with a baffling number of settings and dials to control pressure and angle and who knows what else. While it would be phenomenally useful to master such a tool, it would be phenomenally dangerous to get it wrong. Let's just say I've seen the online photos of hapless apprentices who'd fused their own fingers together.

Next.

The Through and Through put ordinary awls to shame. It was unassuming, to say the least, something like an automotive tire gauge—albeit one with some extra controls on the handle. But the thing that popped out the end was no gauge. It was *pointy*—and it somehow managed to be superheated, superchilled, or super sharp, depending on what needed piercing. Handle it wrong and you'd end up with the Stigmata.

I turned the page, completely overwhelmed. Three choices. *Three.* And every last one of them made me want to give up and try my hand at puppeteering again. And I was a really mediocre puppeteer.

I was so focused on the yellowed pages that I nearly

jumped out of my skin when the door to Hester's workroom banged open. "What on earth did you do to your sweater?" she demanded.

Oh. Right. The hole. "It's kind of a long story."

Hester ducked into her workroom again to grab something, then strode back out to the register with great purpose, cane thumping hard against the floorboards.

"Take it off and put it on the counter."

I blinked. "But what about customers?"

"Do you *see* any customers?"

I didn't. And come to think of it, there hadn't been a single customer since I'd come back from lunch. Oh, we'd had slow days before, but never an entire uninterrupted afternoon. As I wriggled out of my sweater, I glanced surreptitiously at the front of the shop to try and see if I'd somehow locked up behind myself without realizing it. But even if I had, there'd be banging on the door—and probably a tirade of colorful words—if anyone had brought by a repair while I'd been perusing the catalog.

Or...staring at it in befuddlement, if you wanted to be technical.

Eureka waddled out behind her with its metallic tail whispering against the hardwood floor. The half-heard scraping sound always made gooseflesh prickle up and down my arms. And probably other places. Which now made me feel twice as exposed as I stood there, shirtless, in front of Hester and the peacock and whoever else might choose that very moment to drop in.

I crossed my arms and did my best to look like it was just the cold that had me chafing myself, and not nerves, as I cut a glance to the object in Hester's hand. It was roughly the size of a generous meatball. Half of it was clear plastic, half of it gray-flecked melamine, with a chrome band covering the seam between the two materials. It was a similar look to all the other various items on our shelves—a bulbous postwar optimism that clearly marked it as an Apex Magichanical.

"Spread your sweater out on the countertop," she told me. "And line up that hole as best you can."

Once I did as I was told, Hester opened a tiny hatch in the sphere, poked at it a few times, then set the thing down in the middle of the hole.

I waited with bated breath.

Nothing happened.

The peacock let out a startling, "Shkaat!"

Hester picked up the little sphere, held it to her ear, shook it a few times, and placed it back down. It tottered for a moment…and then there was a click.

Spindly mechanical legs shot out from the chrome seams, pointy articulated things. It hadn't been designed to look like a spider—at least, I didn't *think* it had—but as the slender, jointed limbs began poking through the knit, I could hardly think of anything else.

"Apex Hole-be-Gone," Hester said. "From their Happy Homemaker line. Hopefully this Humpty Dumpty won't be too big of a challenge for even the Apex to put back together again."

Ticking and whirring, the magichanical tiptoed forward. Some of the jointed legs had tiny clamps on the ends, almost like a scorpion's claws, while others ended in small metal hooks. The Apex crawled along the shredded yarn, poking and prodding, touching and testing, until it came to a frayed end. It picked up the yarn and fed it into the sphere of its body, humming gently. I could see it through the clear plastic top, twirling around an internal bobbin.

It was a slow process—whatever the little machine was doing—though it did appear to be doing something, given all the ticking and whirring.

"You might as well lock up," Hester said as a bit of blue yarn began to extrude from the back of the Apex spider. "There won't be any customers tonight. Not with the grand opening of Magimart."

Under the scrutiny of the vigilant peacock, I did as I was told.

"That's tonight?" I asked. "I mean, I heard they were coming, but I hadn't realized it would happen quite so soon."

"You can slap a store together pretty darned fast if you're willing to cut corners, do everything the easy way, and work your people to the bone in the process."

The Hole-be-Gone pushed out a few more inches of yarn. While the front end continued to suck in the frayed bits, two of its articulated back feet took up the extruded yarn and began knitting it into the hole.

Hester and I watched for a moment, and then she said, "Were you playing with the Apex Junk Mail Junker?"

"Of course not!" I knew better than to mess around with a magichanical that could chew through a phone book in no time flat. "I was just looking at the auxiliars and one thing led to another—"

Hester looked up sharply. "An auxiliar! Since when are you interested in auxiliars?"

Since I got the bright idea of having it make my decisions for me. *That* answer would go over really well. "I've been puttering around the fringes of magichanical repair long enough. I want to get to the next level—"

"And you think an auxiliar will take you there? Well, I have news for you. Auxiliars are not pets."

"I never said they were—"

"You can't just scratch them behind the ears, toss them a bowl of kibble and call it a day. An auxiliar is an intelligent, sentient creature. Smarter than you, most likely."

"That's why they're so helpful—"

"Everyone thinks they can just traipse in and buy themselves an auxiliar like it's a puppy or a kitten." Well, even if I had harbored those notions, my experience now told me different. But Hester was on a real roll. "An auxiliar is a partner. A partner for life. So, mark my words. You'd be better off picking up some floozy at the bus station and having a drive-through wedding in Vegas than just grabbing the first auxiliar you see and expecting it to all work out."

Our eyes went to the foil peacock...who was clucking to itself as it picked a piece of trim free from the wainscoting.

Hester narrowed her eyes. "At least you can divorce the floozy."

The trim came free with a brittle snap and the peacock let out a pleased metallic chirp.

"All right, already," Hester told the thing, "we're leaving." She nodded toward the Hole-Be-Gone, which was still tick-tocking its way down the sweater, and told me, "You'll want to stay until it's done. If you leave it to its own devices, you might find yourself with a dozen potholders instead of a sweater come morning."

"It doesn't have an automatic shut-off?"

Apparently, that was the wrong thing to say. "Spoken just like a millennial! Always looking for the easy fix, the shortcut, the lazy way out. There is no magic button!"

"But I just wondered—"

"That's the reason this whole world is going to pot. Microwave dinners and disposable cameras. Why spend the time restoring a vintage magichanical? Buy some cheap piece of trash at Magimart, and when it stops working, just throw it away."

I watched the little yarn spider turn a corner and start down another row. "Magimart is just new," I said. "Once they've seen it and satisfied their curiosity, our customers will be back."

I guess that wasn't much comfort. With a parting harrumph, Hester grabbed her cane and thumped out the front door, followed closely by her discomfiting metallic bird.

The shop felt quiet with them gone...quiet-*er*, anyhow. Given that I was still shirtless, it was kind of a relief to be alone, and I didn't mind sticking around to keep the Hole-Be-Gone on track.

I went back to the catalog and paged through it again, trying to imagine which outcome I was most prepared to handle: being spun around, stuck together, or pierced through. And then I wondered if I was really ready to start my apprenticeship after all, if each of the tools filled me with a sense of impending doom.

At my elbow, the Hole-Be-Gone made a little *gronk* sound and started picking its way up the front of the sweater, searching for another yarn end to feed into its spindle. I plucked it off gingerly, located the tiny button, and clicked it off. The articulated legs folded in on themselves and sucked back into the body, and the machine fell silent.

Chilled, I pulled the sweater over my head—and just in

time. A rap at the front window startled me. I looked up and found Jeff peering in with his hands cupped around his eyes. I let him in before he could put any more smudges on my window.

"Aren't you ready to go yet?" he demanded. I smoothed the front of my sweater to demonstrate how it was no longer stretched out...but Jeff didn't notice. "I want to get to Pasta Palace before all the good tables are taken."

Pasta? I felt bloated already. With a sigh, I closed the catalog and slipped it back onto the shelf.

———————•●•·———————

The next morning, the girl with the finger tattoos actually did say more than three words to Jeff. Something to do with which Starship Enterprise was superior—and not in a friendly way, either. But since Jeff didn't seem to care which way he rubbed the poor cashier so long as he got under her skin, I left them to their rather heated discussion and headed toward the shop deep in thought.

Did it really matter which tool I chose? It wasn't as if it would be the only tool I could ever master...just the one I'd be focused on the next five to ten years of my training. Or more.

I was so lost in my own rumination, I hadn't realized I was approaching the auxiliar shop until an unfamiliar voice said, "Penny for your thoughts."

I looked up and—holy smokes—leaning there in the entry alcove was the guy. With the cheekbones. And the clingy white T-shirt. And the most fascinating eyes I'd ever seen...a muted grayish green, like a translucent slice of jade, or the tide coming in.

He smiled...and I forgot how to breathe.

"They still say that," he asked. "Don't they?"

"I...uh...no, just...sorry, I was, um—" Smooth. "I've got a lot on my mind, is all."

"I've been told I'm a good listener," he said, and gestured toward the shop door for me to join him inside.

He wanted to talk. To me. But as I turned to follow him in, a familiar clop-clop reached my ears as Hester rounded one of the three corners, punishing the sidewalk with her brass-tipped cane as Eureka pranced along beside her. If I was late—or less than five minutes early—she might very well change her mind entirely about beginning my apprenticeship.

"Maybe we can talk over dinner," I blurted out, before I could weigh the pros and cons of doing something so ridiculously overconfident. "Like a date," I added, while my brain struggled to catch up with my mouth.

The clerk looked puzzled for a moment...and then intrigued. "Like a date," he repeated as he lavished his secret smile on me.

7

RUNE

"I've just received the most interesting proposition," I told Helix, who was currently busy examining a stray bit of blue yarn.

"If it's anything to do with investing in cryptocurrency, don't fall for it."

"We should definitely table that discussion, as it sounds fascinating. But that's not it. I've been invited out on a date."

Helix looked up from her string and blinked her odd-colored eyes. "By a person?"

"Not only that—but a distinctly male person."

Helix failed to be suitably impressed. "Everybody's dating everybody these days. Heck, you can even marry him if the mood takes you."

I didn't allow her lack of enthusiasm to deter me. "I'd always found people's mating rituals to be so passive. The coy looks. The subtle flirtation. The innuendo. This invite was so refreshingly assertive. So, what do you think...will there be a shared ice cream soda involved? Slow-dancing? How about necking?"

"I think you'd better have another look at the internet before you go."

"More YouTube?"

"Not exactly."

Several hours later, I closed the laptop and sat back with a sigh. I'd had no idea there were so many ways to mash together two (or more) sets of genitals. At the very least, it gave me hope that if I were to try anything that got lost in translation, I could just claim it was my own personal kink.

A few of the other hopefuls drifted in and out of the office as I did my research, though since they had no dates of their own, they regarded the pornography with only passing curiosity. When I finally emerged from the office, though, I found myself subject to a bevy of concerned looks.

"I'm a quick study," I reassured the other auxiliars. "I'm sure I'll do great."

The six-legged meerkat waggled one of its many tiny fingers at me. "That's the problem, Rune. We figured out who this 'date' of yours is. You're taking unfair advantage."

"Of my date?" I asked, baffled.

"Of us," said the foxy moth from its perch on the crown molding. "That was no random passer-by you've insinuated yourself upon." I'd done no such thing...though the night was still young. "That was a customer."

"A customer who left empty-handed," grumbled the rhino.

The meerkat crossed two sets of arms. "You're poaching, is what you're doing. Luring a potential counterpart away from the rest of us so he has no choice but to settle on you."

"I'm not—I wouldn't."

The platypus said, "You're trying to tell us you had no idea that man was a customer?"

"How would he?" Helix snapped. "He was asleep the entire time."

I dusted some cat hair off the front of my dungarees. "This is a real quandary. Of course I don't want to be unsportsmanlike. But if I ditch my date, I'll make us all look bad." It was a thin argument at best, so I added, "How about this? I'll be a person the entire time—and I'll avoid the topic of auxiliars entirely."

The others weren't thrilled about it, I could tell. But they couldn't exactly forbid me to go.

At half-past five, a hush fell over Helping Hands as the door to the tinker shop across the lane opened and my date stepped out. After a brief squabble with the man from the chemist down the block, he squared his shoulders and marched purposefully across the street.

He looked nervous. And also adorable. The puppy-hopefuls could learn a thing or two from him.

I dodged our sales clerk, skirted the dubious looks of a handful of worried auxiliars, and joined my date on the walkway. "I'm Ryan," I declared, since everyone agreed my real name would be a dead giveaway.

The person—Conrad—didn't seem to think anything of it, so I guess the others had steered me right. He suggested we walk. By all means. He admitted he didn't own a car. Well, neither did I. And he said Three Corners had a special place in his heart anyhow...though it would be a relief to eat somewhere other than "that nasty food cart."

He'd lost me there...but it hardly mattered. I'd been

cocooned inside that dusty old shop for so long, I'd forgotten how exhilarating the outside world could be. The air had a fresh nip to it, the traffic lights looked festive, and everything felt incredibly vital and alive.

"Any particular place you'd like to go?" Conrad asked as we strolled along.

I scanned the street, noting that the only mundane business that hadn't changed during my most recent nap was the barber shop down the block. "Why don't you pick?" I suggested.

Conrad stopped in his tracks. I thought at first there was some technological reason to blame: a force field, or a random gravity fluctuation. But it appeared the cause of the pause was nothing quite so futuristic. "The burger place has good fries—are you a vegetarian? No? Okay...but then there was that one incident with the moldy bun. And the deli has great pickles, but they're pretty picked over by this time of day...."

"Wherever we go, it will be a night to remember," I assured him. He laughed nervously, taking it for hyperbole. If people are willing to be convinced, they'll rationalize most anything. I paused outside a shop with cheerful music piping through the door and peered at the sign. Tico's Tacos. "How about tacos? They sound so exotic."

Conrad laughed again, and I laughed right along with him—not because I got the joke, but because it hardly mattered, so long as we were both having fun. The menu was filled with things I'd never heard of, and the value of currency had evidently shifted by two decimal points since I'd last touched money. And here I'd thought the twenty-dollar bill Helix entrusted me with was excessive.

"I'll have what he's having," I announced to the cashier.

"But you don't know what I'm getting," Conrad said.

I shrugged happily. "Then you'd better make it good!"

Combo platter three didn't sound nearly as intriguing as Enchiladas Con Queso, but I supposed it would let me try a little bit of everything. And Conrad wouldn't hear of me paying. Even once I assured him I did have money.

We set down our trays in view of a self-serve soda jerk machine—fascinating—and when my date spread a paper napkin over his lap, I did the same. "I didn't realize you'd have such an oddball sense of humor," he said. "It must come in handy, dealing with customers. Have you been at the auxiliar shop long?"

I tore my eyes away from the ice-clunking, pop-spitting wonder, locked eyes with Conrad, and said, "Let's not talk about work."

"O...kay. Then what do you want to...?"

"Anything. Anything at all," I proclaimed. Conrad looked doubtful, but I truly meant what I said. "Whether you prefer ketchup or mustard. How old you were when you learned how to whistle. If you recall your dreams in the morning. Or how many tries it took you to learn to juggle."

I'd hoisted my plastic utensils as I spoke—they certainly were lightweight nowadays—and they hovered just over my "taco." But luckily for me, I'd been too busy flapping my gums to dig in. Conrad picked his up and ate it with his hands—as did everyone else in the establishment. I followed suit.

Once he swallowed, Conrad said, "I didn't realize the juggling thing was so obvious."

"Lucky guess."

"It was because of a magichanical, actually. Don't worry, I promise this isn't work-related. My cousin had an Apex Jugglo-matic—did you know Apex made toys from 1949 to 1951? Not as profitable as small appliances and home goods, I guess, but there still are a few floating around out there. If only I could get my hands on one to see what made it tick.... Oh. Uh, sorry. I guess I am talking shop after all." His fair cheeks pinked a bit. Human physiology—so intriguing. "Anyway, I wanted to prove that I could do better with my own two hands."

"And could you?"

"Sure...with about a year of practice. At least." A self-deprecating smile. "Not exactly my most profitable skill."

"Even so, I admire a man who knows what he wants."

Conrad's blush deepened.

Was I coming on too strong? Both Helix and the internet had assured me that courting rituals were more straightforward these days than they'd been in centuries, and asking me to dinner was in all likelihood a precursor of asking me to bed. But I appreciated that not all the illicit thrill had been worn away by the passage of time.

Unfortunately, it seemed that his blush had nothing to do with my flirtation. "But that's the thing, Ryan." What? Oh, yes. That's me. "I think I know what I want. I yearn for it so badly, it eats me up from the inside out. But then it comes time to really commit, and I'm like a deer in headlights."

"It's okay if you don't want to invite me back to your place," I said softly. "It was an adventure nonetheless."

"What? No! Of course I want to...that is, if you want to...." He face-palmed. "Sorry...I was actually talking about work. Again."

"Well, what a relief—I was starting to worry you didn't find me half as interesting as I find you."

"Are you kidding? I've never met anyone like you."

Then I should probably be trying a bit harder to fit in. After all, I'd be dreadfully disappointed if we didn't make it through dessert.

8

CONRAD

Ryan was absolutely nothing like I thought he would be, and that was putting it mildly. I'd figured that with those cheekbones, with that tall, effortless grace, he'd be confident. No...to be honest, I thought he'd be a little bit full of himself. Okay, maybe even more than a little. But not only was he unexpectedly funny—he was totally offbeat in a way that made him far more appealing than a chiseled jawline or a set of washboard abs.

Though I *had* gotten a peek at the abs while I was washing the window, and he was no slouch in that department, either.

The walk back to my apartment felt unexpectedly short. Ryan was on an oddball ramble about how surely if the Dick Tracy watch existed, there would be flying cars by now, and I was so wrapped up in it, I didn't have a chance to second-guess myself. A cool guy like him and a dweeb like me, I should have been intimidated. Except Ryan wasn't a cool guy. He was a nerd of the highest order. Heck, he could even put Jeff to shame. And Jeff's prized possession is a mint condition Chewbacca cookie jar that's never once known the touch of so much as a single crumb.

I let him in and we stood there in the unremarkable living room / dining room combo. Unremarkable to me, at least. "That's quite a television set," Ryan said, craning his neck as if to see behind my wall-mounted TV.

"It's only a 40-inch. I keep meaning to replace it when the Black Friday sales roll around, but...." I shrugged.

He made a slow circuit of the room, looking with apparent interest at my lava lamp, my air conditioner, my ancient iMac. "No pets?" he asked.

My hand drifted to my chest, where I could still feel the needle-claws of the Siamese kitten. "Apparently I'm not really an animal person."

"No auxiliar, then?"

"I've thought about it. A lot. But it's such a big decision, and...." I shrugged helplessly. "I'm worried I'd get it wrong." I laughed. I sounded nervous. And also like a goofus who was afraid of auxiliars. "I thought we weren't going to talk shop."

He finished his tour of my underwhelming living space and came to a stop directly in front of me. "We really shouldn't." He smiled his secret smile. "Talking is making it a lot harder for you to kiss me."

Now *there* was an invitation I wouldn't dream of second-guessing. He was close already, and all it took was a half-step forward to press myself against him. He was taller by a good few inches, but a simple tilt of the head was all it took to bring our lips together like they were meant to land just there, and nowhere else. "Funny," I said, when we came up for air. "I kind of figured you'd be the one to kiss *me*."

"I hope you don't mind taking the lead." Ryan cupped my face and ran the pad of his thumb along my jaw, where my five o-clock shadow was settling in. "This is all a little new to me."

Ho. Lee. Crap. Hopefully my jaw didn't literally drop, given that it was resting in his hand. No wonder he'd looked so surprised when I blurted out the world's most awkwardly impulsive dinner invitation. I'd managed to proposition a straight guy.

Straight-*ish*, anyhow...given the way he was staring at my lips with a smoldering look in his enchanting gunmetal green eyes. I leaned in for another kiss, and this time his tongue skimmed across my lower lip with a teasing promise.

Really, not so straight at all.

Between heads, arms, legs and everything in between, there's just so much that can go wrong in a kiss. But not only did our noses find their best fit and our teeth scrape by with just a hint of a clash, but everything else fit together like two Apex gears. I slid one hand around the back of Ryan's neck, threading my fingers through the hair at the nape. My other hand went to his waist, where he was all taut, lean muscle.

Feeling bold, I slid my hand around farther, resting it just above the slope of his ass. He made a happy sound against my mouth. I could hardly believe my good fortune. But I wasn't going to examine it too closely and second-guess away my chance at making his first guy-on-guy encounter a good one.

My hand slid lower and I chanced a squeeze. I felt a smile form against my lips, one that urged me to keep on going. Ryan felt incredible, but he'd feel even better skin to skin. I slipped a hand beneath his T-shirt, fully intending to check in and ask if that was all right—but his breath hissed in, a cool tickle against my lower lip, and it was so clear that he wanted me to keep on going, pausing to ask would only have busied my mouth with something way more forgettable than our kisses.

We only stopped kissing long enough to pull off our shirts. His nimble hands explored every exposed inch of me—even parts I hadn't realized were particularly interesting, like the crooks of my elbows and the hollow of my throat. Maybe the boldness to take stock of what he was experiencing was something that only came with age. (He was maybe, what— thirty? Probably. Though he had a way about him that made him seem both younger and, paradoxically, older.)

My own first time, I was a pimply fifteen-year-old who took Truth or Dare a lot farther than either me or the other kid had intended. Neither of us actually *came* in that dark coat closet...but the first time I'd had a dick jammed in my mouth left a pretty big impression, nonetheless.

An impression of utter awkwardness.

Both of us tasted like Doritos and Mountain Dew. He'd stepped on my foot hard enough to leave me limping. I'd nearly poked his eye out. And the scrape of my braces on his most sensitive part nearly sent him into orbit.

If that first tentative BJ in the coat closet was the first few notes of a melody, this thing I was doing with Ryan wasn't just a harmony...it was a symphony. Though a music metaphor really didn't do it justice. No, as we flowed toward the bedroom, touching and kissing, it felt more like a mint condition Apex magichanical, one where every spring, cog and lever was so pristine it could click along forever.

It was only when the backs of my legs butted up against the mattress that my confidence began to erode. Being someone's first anything is a huge deal—because you always remember your first time, and I'd hate to be Ryan's unfortunate Truth or Dare.

I slid my mouth from his and said, "If you want, we could just do hand stuff."

"Is that so?" His secret smile was back...broader than before. "I think we should do *all* the stuff. If you're game, that is."

Was he kidding? *Game* was practically busting out of my jeans. He tipped me back on the bed and stripped me the rest of the way down, and somehow we still flowed together like we'd been choreographed. If it weren't for Ryan's occasional pause to stop and look, touch or taste (as if he was committing everything to memory), I would never have believed his claim about never having done this with a man before. Then again, I suppose when you got right down to it, a body is still a body, and only a few specifics are entirely different.

Speaking of which...his specifics were rock hard and raring to go.

I, technically, might have been the one calling the shots. But we were so simpatico, Ryan moved with me as if he was reading my mind. When I wanted to touch him, his hand wrapped around me like the idea had just occurred to him as well. And when I couldn't decide whether to get a good taste of him or lose myself to the pleasure I'd bungled in the coat closet, we shifted in opposite directions to something less of a 69 and more of a yin-yang.

It was hard to think analytically with his mouth sliding over me so painfully perfect...but the taste of him was nothing like anyone I'd ever been with. Hints of salt and musk were there, but underlying that was a smell that wasn't entirely chemical or animal or magichanical, but a combination of every enchanted element that might fire a young boy's imagination. The smell of Three Corners.

Which led me to wonder exactly how long he'd been working there. It hardly seemed like you could wear Three Corners on your skin in just a short amount of time. Maybe he'd been across the street from me all along, and I'd just been too wrapped up in myself to notice. I could hardly stop what I was doing and ask, though. Not with Ryan making those broken little sounds of pleasure around my dick.

It seemed like we might finish each other that way, but when I felt the first inklings of my brink approaching, Ryan paused and said, "What about the 'stuff' where you're inside me...can we do that, too?"

Wow, talk about *all* the stuff.

He watched me put on my condom with interest. Maybe straight guys just think about them as birth control—or maybe he expected me to make some weird excuse about it dulling the sensation and talk him into letting me bareback.

Huh. Maybe I wasn't such a bad first-gay-hookup after all.

I took things slow and careful. The wincing, cringing, just-gimme-a-second responses I'd concerned myself with never materialized. In fact, I might've had a hard time believing that Ryan wasn't an old pro. Then again, he hadn't been super specific about what, exactly, was so new to him. For all I knew, he did straight butt stuff all the time.

My peak had receded when we first changed positions and I slowed everything down to make sure *ooh yeah* didn't turn into *oh ouch*. But pretty soon it was *ooh yeah* all the way, and I found an angle and a rhythm that sent us both spiraling toward our bliss.

He came with me inside him, painting an outlandish spurt

of pearlescent satisfaction across his own belly and chest, and I let myself tip over that precipice buried deep. Even once my orgasm receded to an aftershock shiver, I kept position where I was between his legs, wishing I could stay inside him forever so this first time together didn't have to end.

Ryan looped his arms around my neck and pulled me in for a sated kiss...then inquired whether we could switch spots for round two.

All the stuff, indeed.

We reconfigured and found our motion smoothly—so smoothly that I was tempted to challenge the claim that this was all new to him. But it takes two to tango. And it wasn't just Ryan doing everything right, but the two of us somehow responding as if our bodies could anticipate each other on a primal, subconscious level.

It took longer this time around, but in the best possible way. With the need for release less urgent, we could take our time in exploratory thrusts and lazy kisses. But eventually those thrusts grew more focused, the kisses more urgent, and we peaked again, together.

Ryan rolled off me so we could stare up at the ceiling together with his head pillowed on my shoulder. I felt like I should float the idea that I hoped the first-gay-hookup could lead to a first-gay-potential-boyfriend...but I didn't want to scare the guy off by demanding too much, too soon. And so I thought it was best to let him talk first.

Eventually, he said, "Time flies when you're having fun—so how is it still quarter to nine?"

On the wall at the foot of the bed, my Apex clock read its perpetual 8:46. "That clock has been broken ever since I can remember." It belonged to my grandfather. I was named after him—more precisely, my first name's his last name and my middle name his first name. Maybe that's where the bond started. You're not supposed to play favorites with your grandkids...but Grandpa Joe and I were two peas in a pod. He knew I had a thing for magichanicals, and when he passed, he left the clock to me.

"I plan on fixing it," I said.

"Maybe there's something to be said for lingering in the moment." Ryan nestled against the crook of my shoulder and ran a fingertip down my sternum. "Especially when you're having a good time."

I wasn't sure how to take that. Was having a good time a precursor to "let's do this again," or was the whole encounter on par with a great game of mini-golf or a soak in the Jacuzzi? I didn't want to come off too needy, though, so I didn't ask. I'd initiate the second date when the time was right. After breakfast, for instance.

So long as it wasn't at that awful food cart.

People tend to "sleep on it" when they have a big decision to make—though it's never worked for me—but even so, I was confident that it would sound the most natural to suggest date number two when we parted ways in the morning, me to the tinker shop and him to his auxiliars.

Unfortunately, it didn't pan out that way.

I woke to an empty bed. So empty that I knew immediately Ryan was gone. No footfalls or running water or brewing coffee. It was too quiet, too still, for me to be anything but alone. And it could've been that he just wanted to sleep in his own bed, or to grab a shower and a change of clothes before work...except for the possibility that he was maybe not quite as bisexual as he initially thought, and couldn't deal with the walk of shame when it was coming from the apartment of another man.

I looked around to see if maybe he'd left a note, but no, there was nothing to show for our evening but a phenomenally rumpled bed.

9

RUNE

I could have slept for days. Not because I was exhausted—being with Conrad had been surprisingly energizing—but because his bed was so much cozier than a dusty wooden shelf. I luxuriated in the cool sheets, extending my limbs one at a time as I eased into wakefulness. When memories of the night before started tickling the edges of my awareness, though, I jerked fully awake, momentarily panicked over changing forms when I dozed off. That sort of thing is generally pretty startling to someone who doesn't own an auxiliar. But since I'd heard no screaming, presumably I'd done so sometime after Conrad got up.

Crisis averted.

The sheets I was tangled in smelled of our delightful tussle from the night before. Good thing I'd watched all those sexy videos and absorbed the proper mechanics. Spurting in tandem with Conrad had definitely been the highlight of the evening. In fact, I was eager to do it again and try out one of the many positions I'd seen on the website. Hopefully he was up for another go, himself.

I listened for a moment, but didn't hear my fine bedfellow. A glance at the clock told me it was still quarter to nine—in some reality, at least—but a glance out the window showed it was closer to noon. He'd be at his shop by now, so I supposed I was alone.

He'd let me sleep in. How thoughtful!

According to whatever unspoken rules I'd picked up on, it was my turn to take the initiative, and I shouldn't waste any time in arranging our next date. I congratulated myself for taking note of the name of his shop. Now all I had to do was ask the operator to connect me....

Except there was no telephone to call him with. Of course not. His phone would be in his pocket.

I made a mental note to catch up with Conrad later, then. Once I'd had some coffee. And a nice shower. And enjoyed a show or two on his massive (yet impossibly thin) television set.

The new coffee machines were a lot trickier than the percolators I remembered, but I managed. All the towels I tried out were delightfully soft. And animation had come a long way, particularly the special effects. But soon the commercials grew tiresome. Once I'd seen the fourth or fifth prescription drug ad, I decided it was time to head home.

I slipped into the shop intending to tell Helix all about my first date with a human, at least until she started making hairball noises when I got to the steamy parts...but when I closed the door behind me, my entire mood shifted.

Helping Hands was thrumming with anxiety. Not the shop itself, which was nothing more than timbers and plaster, but the dozens of hopefuls who called the place home—and they were *emanating* dread. I followed the unease like a trail of breadcrumbs, through the shelves and into the showroom, where the auxiliars all huddled together, whispering among themselves.

While the rhino paced in a very tight circle, the cat who walked on her hind legs only was wringing her front paws together in a very matronly way. She was saying, "It's ridiculous to think that anyone would want an auxiliar when they can get an inanimate object at Magimart for a fraction of the price. One that won't saddle anyone with its bothersome opinions..." she glanced up at the fox-faced moth. "Or wreak havoc with the light fixtures."

Helix caught my eye and slunk over to where I stood, lashing me with her tail as she circled my feet. "Well, look what the cat dragged in. About time. Everyone's having conniptions about Magimart. Why don't you talk some sense into them?"

Everyone looked at me expectantly. I chose my words carefully so they couldn't accuse me of taking unfair advantage. "Obviously, I didn't say anything about being an auxiliar...but it seemed to me that Conrad had a healthy respect for tradition."

The meerkat scoffed. "I told you all he was just trying to butter the guy up for a sale."

Oh, I'd buttered him up, all right. But since they were all being so defensive, I wasn't about to treat them to the juicy details. "He'd never believe any of us could be replaced by a self-watering plastic plant or three-way salt and pepper shaker. And if Conrad truly gets it, then others must feel the same."

I strode to the center of the group in my two-legged person-form, spread my arms wide, and said, "I've been outside

Three Corners, and the world has changed. We need to change with it. Not the essence of what we are, but the way we go about connecting with our partners. Our counterparts may not have thought to seek us out here, in this dusty little shop. But we have access to the internet. We could put up a billboard—or even make a TV commercial. People are barraged by advertisements nowadays. It's no wonder they've forgotten about us if no one's reminding them we exist. It'll take some elbow grease and gumption, but I have no doubt that if this shop does close down, each and every one of us can find our perfect home before the doors close for good."

The auxiliars all stared at me for a long moment—it was the most I'd said in ages—but then fell right back into their chattering predictions that the sky was falling, and before we knew it, they'd all be out on their furry, scaly or warty asses.

10

CONRAD

I glanced up through my smudgy storefront window for the umpteenth time, hoping to catch a glimpse of Ryan, but no dice. The longer I had to think, the more I second-guessed the wisdom of going over there. Would I seem too clingy if I just stopped in to say hi?

Clearly, last night I should have said something about wanting to see him again, but I'd overthought everything (as usual) and missed my chance. Maybe he thought I wasn't into it. Maybe that was why he'd left.

Although the window wasn't on my to-do list from Hester, I spent the entire morning squeegeeing it within an inch of its life. Okay, mainly I was staring at the shop window across the street, but the squeegee made for a convenient excuse. Unfortunately, I didn't see anything other than a tiger-striped cat that occasionally popped up to keep an eye on the sidewalk.

Lunchtime, I decided. I'd march right over there and tell him I'd like to see him again. No weird pretense. No elaborate preamble. Just put it all on the table and see if he felt the same.

The worst he could say was no.

Even the mere thought of that was upsetting beyond belief.

But I had to try.

I was so geared up for the conversation—or, more accurately, ill with nerves—that I didn't even see Jeff coming until I walked right into him on the sidewalk. Papers went flying like we were tiny little characters in a freshly shaken snow globe. "What the hell, Conrad, walk much?"

"Geez, sorry, I..." we both started grabbing up the fallen paper before it blew into the street. "I guess I wasn't looking."

"Well, I've got something you'll *really* want to see." He grabbed the papers from me, shuffled them around, then thrust them back under my nose.

"A...job application?"

"A Magimart job application," he said eagerly.

"But I don't want—"

"Health insurance? 401k? Stock options?"

This was probably not the time to admit I wasn't entirely clear what stock options were. "I don't know that I'm the best fit for retail."

"There's more to working at Magimart than just being a greeter—and anyhow, I think the toothless old guy from the gas station's got dibs on that job. They need customer service reps. Managers. A whole marketing team. Once you get your foot in the door, the only way is up!"

Normally, the thought of doing something collaborative and creative and getting paid a bunch of money for it might have had some appeal. But all I could think about was the look in Ryan's haunting green-gray eyes when he glanced down at my mouth just before he pressed his lips to mine.

Unfortunately, Jeff doesn't take no for an answer. And

by the time I finally agreed to fill out the application, our lunch break was over. I briefly considered popping across the street anyway, but spotted Eureka casting a baleful metallic eye on me from the other side of my sparkling clean window.

I headed back to my register and stuck the job application in the cubbyhole beneath it. I didn't notice the normal chipping, filing, grinding sounds were absent from Hester's workroom until I was alerted to her approach by the unmistakeable sound of her cane.

"Well, Conrad, are you done trying to get that window clean enough to eat off of?"

I glanced down at the application, then quickly back. "It's, um...yes?"

"Because I have it on good authority that most foods won't stick to a vertical surface anyway."

It took a second for me to realize that Hester had been making a joke.

I nearly pinched myself to see if I was dreaming...except I'd tried that before and still found myself being chased by a snapping turtle the size of a pop-up camper, so clearly that wouldn't work.

A few clomps brought Hester to my side. She reached into the cubby beneath the register, and my heart stuttered. She knew about the Magimart application—and now I could kiss my job at Arti-fix goodbye. But before I could stammer out some fake-sounding truth about only taking the thing to get rid of Jeff, her hand closed over the dog-eared catalog instead. She slapped it down on the countertop and said, "You've been studying. Have you made your decision?"

I blinked stupidly.

"What's it going to be?" she asked. "The Through 'n Through, the Rejoinder, or the Spintastic?"

"It's...well, I was just...it seems like they all have their pros and cons and I'm not sure...."

From behind us came a metallic grumble that sounded like, "Nrnovm."

"I haven't got all day," Hester said.

I closed my eyes, hoping beyond hope that a ten-foot-tall snapping turtle could make an appearance and save me this utter discomfort. But, no. I was awake. "I just need a little more time to figure it out," I said softly—but Hester had already whirled around with a disgusted sniff to clomp-clomp back into her workroom.

Just imagine, I thought, how much worse it would have been if she'd seen the Magimart application. I folded it up and crammed it into my pocket.

Hester spent the rest of the day sequestered behind that door, leaving me to the customers, and my guilt, and my growing apprehension that I'd blown my chance with Ryan by not speaking up and telling him how I felt. I was counting down the moments till closing time when a customer strode in with a shopping bag on her arm...and I recognized the owner of the knock-off picture frame.

At least she didn't have her spitty kid with her today.

Still, dread washed over me even as she plunked a Magimart bag on the counter.

"I'd like to return this," the customer said testily, and pulled a funny-looking cell phone charger out of the bag.

"You can't do that here."

"It stopped working and I haven't even had it two days. It must be under warranty."

"I'm sure that's possible, but you'd need to return it wherever you bought it."

The woman spat out an exasperated huff. "The customer service line at Magimart is at least two dozen people deep. I'd be there for hours."

"We don't sell new magichanical items here," I said, trying my best to be patient. "We repair them."

"Then *fix* it," she snapped, and stomped out the door.

And that was the last straw. I was sick and tired of people walking all over me. I had to start standing up for myself. "I need a break," I called over my shoulder, and without waiting for Hester to come out and start complaining about millennials these days and their work ethic, turned over the *Be Back Soon!* sign and locked up the shop. I spotted the customer climbing into her car, but it wasn't her I was after. It was Ryan.

I strode across the street, filled with resolve. I'd tell him I wanted to see him again. And if he didn't feel the same, at least I'd know I tried.

The shop door opened with a tinkle, and the smell hit me—that odd, dry scent, like ancient potpourri that had given up nearly all of its fragrance, but still retained the slightest hint of flower petals and amber.

Ryan's smell.

My stomach did a few nervous flip-flops, but I knew if I didn't speak up for myself now, chances were, I never would. And so I looped up and down the labyrinthian aisles, steeling myself at every corner for the probability that I'd soon be faced with the guy who'd rocked my world, then quietly slipped off into the night.

With each aisle, I tensed up harder, sure that any moment

I'd turn a corner and find him standing there looking even better than I remembered. But as I came toward the last aisle, another, more problematic, thought occurred to me: Ryan might not be there at all.

And as I rounded the final corner, I came upon the middle-aged clerk seated at a desk with his mustache and shiny bald head. He tapped something into a laptop, and I realized I'd gotten myself all worked up for nothing. "Excuse me," I said, and the man looked up, startled. "Is Ryan here?"

He looked puzzled.

"Ryan," I repeated, as if maybe I hadn't articulated it well enough the first time. Still no recognition. "The other guy who works here."

The man stood, looking slightly chagrined. "I'm sorry, there must be some mistake. I'm the only one who works here."

I was backing away already even as he spoke, feeling weirdly untethered, like a balloon sliding from the grasp of my own hand and floating away. Ryan had to work here. I saw him rolling up the blinds.

He smelled like the shop.

As my mouth worked helplessly, trying to figure out how to convince the clerk that surely there was a Ryan here—one he just hadn't happened to cross paths with day in, day out, working in the same damn shop for who-knows-how-long, he said, "Oh, I remember you! Have you changed your mind about getting an auxiliar? I apologize for the sweater incident, but it's a hazard of the trade. But I can offer you a small discount to make up for it if you do decide to buy."

Something bumped my ankle as he spoke. I looked down and found a rabbit staring up at me with huge, limpid eyes.

Its fur was a misty gray, all but a tiny tuft of white between its floppy ears. "You have rabbits?" I said stupidly.

"The form of an auxiliar is malleable," the clerk assured me. "A good auxiliar is responsive to the needs of its counterpart. And since kittens really weren't your style...."

A fox wove briefly between my calves, then planted itself to one side, gazing up at the overhead light. A guinea pig peeped out from beneath a low shelf and clucked at me expectantly. And a stately-looking toad chirruped a surprisingly melodic tune from a nearby tabletop. Not a single kitten to be seen.

Except for the bony black cat glaring at me from a high shelf behind the clerk's head. Now that I was up close, I saw it had one blue eye and one yellow. I pointed urgently. "That cat. That's Ryan's auxiliar."

"Helix?" The clerk shook his head regretfully. "No, she's quite available, I assure you."

With the same sort of disdain I'd come to expect from our resident peacock, the cat raised a paw and deliberately knocked something off the shelf. Nearly overbalancing, the clerk caught it and put it on the counter.

It was the greenish, grayish lump I'd noticed last time. A cactus, maybe. Or an invertebrate of some kind. "What's that even supposed to be, anyhow?"

"No one really knows. It's dormant. But don't worry, we still have plenty of active auxiliars to choose from. One of them is bound to be your perfect counterpart."

I had the urge to pick the thing up and turn it in my hands, to see if it was pliant or hard, warm or cool...to raise it up to my face and smell it. But before I could reach for the thing, the clerk snatched it up and stuck it in his desk drawer. "How about a nice koala?"

"I'll think about it," I said (with absolutely no intention of doing so), and headed back across the street with a heavy heart.

CONRAD

I'd expected Hester to read me the riot act for ditching Arti-fix without permission, but when I got back to my post, I found her standing at the counter with her auxiliar at her feet and her spare toolbox in her hands. "Conrad, you've got the worst case of analysis paralysis I've ever seen," she said without preamble. "I've given it some thought, and I suspect that the more you research the tools, the less likely you are to pick one."

"Trime!" the metal peacock screamed.

I wiped my damp palms against the leg of my pants. "What if you just demonstrated them one more time?"

"This again?" Hester sighed. "I've shown you their workings umpteen times. It's time you tried one on for size."

The thought of accidentally twisting apart a genuine Apex magichanical made me lightheaded. "Not with an actual Apex...." I found the cell phone charger the irate customer had left behind. "But maybe on something like this."

Hester snatched the charger from me and scowled at it through the crescents of her bifocals. "This is no real magichanical."

"I didn't say it was—"

"I'll show you what happens when you try to repair something that was never meant to be fixed." Hester snapped her fingers, and Eureka ducked into the workroom and came back with a Pryer Engagement—a metal apparatus with a variety of blunted blades that snapped open like the fan of a flamenco dancer. An expert flick of Hester's arthritic wrist sent the tiny prybars dancing across the seam of the charger's housing. With a clickety tick, the tool tapped against the shell with each slender metal tongue until, finally, one eked its way past the seal and pried the case open.

My breath caught. The workings of a magichanical are always a sight to behold. Gears and pulleys, switches and springs—none of them assembled quite like you'd expect, but somehow one part always manages to click with the other, tick-tocking along in a carousel of magichanical wonder. I leaned in eagerly, wondering what, exactly, I'd see—

Then flinched back in dismay as Hester tipped up the charger's housing...and poured out a pile of sand.

"Electrosilica," she said with disdain—it was a common magical agent. "Capable of holding a charge or two, but without true magichanical parts topping up the charge with some good, old-fashioned friction, there's no way for it to keep on sparking."

While I stared dumbly, Hester swept the pile of inert sand into the trash, and then slid the spare toolbox my way. "Take the tools home with you, Conrad. None of them should be lethal—so long as you aim the Through and Through *away* from you, anyhow. Hold them. Turn them on. But most importantly, try them out. I don't care what you practice on, so long as I don't get a call from the emergency room.

But by Monday morning, you'll tell me where to begin your training."

At closing time, Jeff tried to lure me to the movies, but I told him to go without me. He has no problem going solo—he just likes to eat all my popcorn. "Don't you even want to know what's playing?" he called after me...but I didn't. I had work to do.

The toolbox couldn't have weighed more than a few pounds, but it grew heavier and heavier as I made my way home. There was a strong possibility I wouldn't be able to make up my mind even after handling them—and what then? Go fight the toothless guy from the gas station over the greeter job at Magimart?

Or maybe the real reason I couldn't get excited about the tools was the fact that Ryan ghosted me.

I approached my apartment with a pall of gloom hanging over my head, sure I was doomed to drift through life like a shadow of my true self, directionless, alone and perpetually undecided. But all that self-pity fell away the moment I put my key in the lock and, before I actually unlocked it, my door swung open.

I froze...and listened. The TV was on, with the weatherman predicting a forty percent chance of rain, followed by some dumb banter with the news anchor that segued to a commercial for a local used car lot. *Call the cops*, my common sense told me. But a peek through the gap in the door showed my dining room was trashed, and I was gripped by a fear even greater than the thought of being clobbered by the burglar I was about to surprise—the fear that if I didn't do something *now*, Grandpa Joe's Apex clock would be smashed to smithereens.

Before I could talk myself out of it, I'd fallen back a few paces and opened up my toolbox. I grabbed hold of the Through 'n Through, holding it out in front of me like a shank in a prison fight. It might've looked like a fancy orange reamer, but even the dumbest criminal would know better than to mess with a desperate guy wielding a magichanical tool.

I eased through my door, though I really didn't need to be all that sneaky. My footsteps would've been camouflaged by the sports scores being rattled off by the newscaster. Even so, I crept in carefully, skirting my kitchenette, also trashed. What the heck—my robber stopped to make himself a freaking sandwich? That was just adding insult to injury. I peeked in the bathroom. Empty...though there were wet towels everywhere. And finally, I came to the bedroom.

The clock was hanging right where it always was, hands at their usual 8:46.

No robber.

Not now, at any rate. But he'd definitely been there. Sure, I'd left the sheets rumpled...not thrown around the room like a tornado hit the bed. A few shirts were even tossed over the mattress as if someone had been *trying on my things*. I chafed away goosebumps, feeling violated and gross. Thankfully I didn't blow myself full of holes with the Through 'n Through.

When I could finally speak without my voice shaking, I did call the cops. They sent someone over to take a statement—a cool and efficient woman who jotted some notes, then suggested I call my insurance company. I didn't tell her I'd never really considered renter's insurance, not when my prized possession was irreplaceable. And I double-locked my door once she left, sat down at my messy dining room table, put my head in my hands...and wondered how my life had come to this.

A clock that would stay broken because I couldn't choose a tool.

A guy I'd never see again because I'd second-guessed myself about telling him how I felt.

An empty life where everyone else kept trying to tell me what I wanted, from my best friend to my parents to the bald guy at the auxiliar shop. And if I didn't stand up for myself now, I'd never get what I wanted.

Rationally, I knew Helping Hands was closed for the night—Three Corners was no Magimart, and everyone shut their doors by dinnertime—but the time for rationality had come and gone. I tore up that damn Magimart application and strode out the door on a full head of steam, walking with long, agitated strides that ate up the pavement.

When I found myself in front of the shop, sure enough, the interior was dark and the blinds were down. I felt ridiculous. What had I expected, anyway? That by some great coincidence, the store would just so happen to be open?

Such an idiot.

I began to turn away...though as I did, I realized that a glint I'd taken for a reflection of a street lamp was actually a tiny light shining out from somewhere deep inside the warren of shelves, glimpsed through the edge of the blinds. There were umpteen possible explanations, from a heat lamp on a reptile's cage to a properly marked emergency exit. But instead of succumbing to my "analysis paralysis," I summoned all my pent-up frustration and disappointment and banged on the front door glass.

A moment later, there was movement inside the shop. A figure approached. Too small to be the clerk—too small to be Ryan. A dark-haired woman around my age, barely five feet tall and painfully thin. The clerk's daughter? Maybe. She wore a strappy, studded plaid dress, ripped fishnets and black nail polish. Her face was mostly in shadow, but even so, I could see her eyeliner was drawn thick. She opened the door. The bells up top gave off a tinkle that was overloud in the nighttime stillness.

"Can I help you?" she said dryly.

No second-guessing. "I want an auxiliar."

"Is that so?"

"Not just any auxiliar, either. I don't want a puppy or a kitten or a rabbit or a fox. There's a greenish-gray, uh...well, I don't know what it is, exactly."

The corner of the woman's mouth quirked. "But you want it all the same?"

"I do."

"Then don't just stand there. Let's find your auxiliar." She turned to walk back into the darkened shop with a swish of her dress, leaving me to follow.

We walked through the showroom, where things I couldn't quite see rustled nervously. But I ignored them—ignored everything but the fact that I was finally doing what *I* wanted for a change. By the light of an open laptop, the dark-haired woman strolled the perimeter of the showroom, dragging her fingertips along the shelves. "Let's see...was it a turtle? Or maybe a sand dollar?" There was a lilt to her voice, like she was just humoring me—that, clearly, I'd flipped my lid.

But I wasn't about to back down now. "Check the desk drawer."

She strolled over to the desk, opened the drawer, and pulled out a pair of reading glasses. A pencil sharpener. A notepad. I was about to knock her out of the way, tear the drawer out of the desk and upend the thing myself when she pulled out something else—something the size of an especially large potato—and held it up to the light of the laptop. "This old thing? Are you sure?"

"Positive."

She inspected it more closely. "I suppose I can let you have it for...twenty."

I'd hoped it wouldn't be quite so steep. "Twenty...thousand?"

"Twenty dollars." She shrugged. "That should settle our debt."

"But it's an *auxiliar.*"

Her face was still mostly in shadow, but I could tell she cracked a grin. "Then you'd better seal the deal before I change my mind."

Since I was positive I was committing grand larceny, I refused to hand over the cash until she'd printed out an official receipt. (Under "auxiliar type," I noted, she'd just entered a few question marks. Hopefully that wouldn't render it null and void.)

The auxiliar was neither warm nor cold, hard nor soft, but it was definitely not inanimate. There was a slight velvety sensation to its skin, and the sense that if I squeezed hard enough, there might be a bit of give.

The woman crossed her arms impatiently. "Are you gonna stand there staring at the darn thing all night or take it home?"

I decided I'd best get out while the getting was good.

I hurried home, so excited about the auxiliar that I actually forgot about the break-in. But when I found myself standing there in my trashed apartment, I wondered what the hell I'd been thinking. I swept aside some dirty dishes and a few stray slices of bread, and set down the greenish-grayish creature on the spot I'd cleared.

"I don't know how much better this is than the inside of a desk drawer." I ran my fingers nervously through my hair. "Hell, I don't know anything at all. Are you hot? Are you cold? Are you hungry—and for that matter, do you even need to eat at all?" I crossed my arms and began to pace around the room, ranting to myself. "See, this is exactly why I don't do impulsive things. If I'd taken a minute to think everything through, I would've realized I'm in way over my head. Great. Just great. Now I have absolutely no idea what you are, what you eat, and whether or not you're even going to survive the weekend."

"That peanut butter of yours wasn't bad...but I suspect I finished it all." I spun around and found Ryan sprawled on his back on my dining room table, knees bent, head hanging down over the edge. "Your ceiling has little sparkles in it, did you know that?"

"Geez, give a guy a heart attack!" I shouted...and then I realized that I had, indeed, locked my door behind me when I came in. "What—? How—? Were you *hiding* somewhere?" It wasn't a big place, but it's not like I'd double-checked behind the shower curtain before I left.

"Of course not. I was with you."

"Holy crap!" I floundered over to the table and shoved him aside. "I think you might've squashed it."

"Now, before you get upset—or any *more* upset—I think we should both take a breath, and keep in mind that when we look back on this someday, we'll both find it quite funny."

"Where did it go?" I shoved him onto his side, expecting to find a grayish-green pancake stuck to his back. Thankfully, there was nothing there but a stray slice of bread. I dropped to my hands and knees to see if he'd knocked the auxiliar under the table, and he gave my butt an encouraging pat. "Ryan," I warned him, "I am so *not* laughing!"

He swung around so he was now sitting on the tabletop with his legs dangling over the side and cracked a rueful grin. "I guess that's as good a place to start as any. My name isn't Ryan—it's Rune."

12

RUNE

In retrospect, lying about one's name may not be the best way to kick off a relationship. "Think of it this way," I told Conrad. "It's really only a difference of a vowel and a consonant. Or maybe two vowels...because, sometimes Y."

"You're an auxiliar." Conrad crossed his arms over his chest—tightly, as if he needed to hold himself together. "So you're actually a weird gray lump?"

"I do wish your scientists had gotten the opportunity to put a name to it. Even if it was a bit overly formal, I'm sure it would sound better than Grayus Lumpus."

"What?"

"Sadly, those creatures were wiped out even before the dinosaurs. And their fossils didn't age well. But that isn't my native form—we don't *have* native forms. It's just the one I've had the most practice with."

"You—I—we *slept* together, and you're not even a person!"

He was awfully cute when he was flustered. "Clearly I am. Or at least I was last night when we did all the stuff." Conrad looked like he was about to hyperventilate, but I couldn't help but add, "If I were in another form, that might be a little odd."

"Oh my god."

"Or maybe just kinky. Depending on how you look at it."

"And when I thought you'd ditched me this morning—you were still somewhere in my bed? The whole time?"

"It's a very comfortable mattress."

"Memory foam," he murmured. But when I slipped off the table and took a step toward him, he squeezed himself tighter and took a matching step back. "Where did your clothes come from? And where do they go when you change shape? Are they even clothes, or are they like part of your skin?"

"You really do have a tendency to overthink things."

He clapped his hands over his mouth and said through his fingers, "When I peeled your shirt off last night, was I—?"

"Conrad." He'd backed into the kitchenette half-wall. I squared myself up with him and took him by both shoulders. "Everything about me—the clothes, the form, even the personality—is an idea. An idea made manifest."

His eyes ticked back and forth as he processed my explanation...which was pretty darned good in its digestibility, if I do say so myself. At any rate, it seemed to calm him down, as his breathing evened out and the color came back to his cheeks. (I made note of this reaction for future use in case I ever had to demonstrate agitation. Though given my easygoing nature, it was unlikely I'd get a chance to use it.)

I gave his shoulders a squeeze, then reached up to skim my fingertips across his cheek. When he didn't flinch away, I eased myself closer, slouching so our bellies brushed. He sucked in a breath.

Not with fear, but desire.

"I'm sorry I didn't give you the whole story," I said softly. "I'd made a promise to the others to keep it under wraps and couldn't go back on my word."

Conrad sighed shakily. "I suppose it could be said of anyone that you don't learn all there is to know about them on the first date." It sounded a bit stilted as he said it...but I appreciated his willingness to try and be understanding.

His gaze fell to my lips, and he said, "So...when you said you hadn't done it before—er, *all the stuff*—did you mean with a *man*, or...?"

I sensed it was not the best time to mention that gender, for us, was also just another flexible idea, given that we could be anything from a hermaphroditic snail to a fungus with thousands of potential sexes. "I've had plenty of counterparts—just as I'm sure you've had plenty of lovers."

"*Plenty* would be kind of a stretch."

"But I've never trailed my tongue across the collarbone of another human." When Conrad let out a small gasp, I added under my breath, "I really like the way you taste."

"And I really like the way you smell," Conrad murmured, ever so subtly leaning in....

When our lips crashed together, his breath caught, cool against my tongue. With each new sensation I noticed, my current form draped itself in the idea. I've always been a convincing person—then again, when people see someone acting strangely, their first thought is usually mental imbalance, instead of "not an actual human"... though maybe they should re-think that.

Conrad's hands fell to my hips, and he thumbed the chiseled vee at my pelvis where it peeked out over my waistband. He broke our kiss and said, "So, you don't actually need to work out to get these muscles."

"Would you rather I ditch them?"

"Well, let's not be hasty."

He led me to the bedroom and ventured another kiss. There was a cautiousness to him, a restraint—or so it seemed at first. But when I opened myself up to the idea of him (because even homo sapiens are part idea) I realized he was simply trying to reassemble what he'd presumed about me before, and see how that knowledge fit with what he now knew.

When I peeled off my shirt and dropped it to the floor, he only spared it a passing concerned look—though he did pause with his lips at the crook of my elbow. "If your body is technically an idea, then does it even matter where I touch you, or is everything fair game?"

I pressed my lips to his ear and said, "Why don't we find out?"

Conrad might have been hesitant at first, but his caution gave way to curiosity. No big surprise. Historically, my counterparts tend to have agile minds with big imaginations. Though none of them had the audacity to drive me wild by sliding their tongues into all my secret places. We sated one another so many times I nearly lost count.

Actually, that's not quite true. He came two times and I did thrice....

"If you had a real human body, you'd need more recovery time," Conrad noted as we sprawled together on the tousled mattress and caught our breath.

I drew a lazy circle with my fingertip on his bare shoulder and considered the observation. "I've seen different on the internet, so we'd have to agree to disagree."

"Yeah...we'll need to have a talk about the credibility of the things you find online. I get the feeling your perspective on certain issues could use a little filling in." Conrad went quiet for a moment, brow furrowing. "Speaking of which...you're welcome to stay—that goes without saying—but I hope you don't feel you have to stick around just because the receipt says so."

"Don't be ridiculous. You're my counterpart. Where else would I want to be?"

CONRAD

I woke the next morning to sunlight knifing through blinds that had been knocked askew, and a twinge in my hamstrings where I'd held a certain position just a bit too long... but no regrets. Not until I realized I was alone.

Or...was I?

Rune's prehistoric form was about as big as a ball of un-risen pizza dough—in other words, something a person would normally notice in their bed. But to say we'd been a little exuberant was putting it mildly. Only one corner of the fitted sheet was still attached, and the rest was wadded between the mattress and the headboard. The comforter was hopelessly tangled with the top sheet. And one of the pillowcases was inside-out and halfway across the room. I was sifting through wreckage when I heard water running in the kitchen. I plucked a pair of boxers off a nearby lamp, pulled them on, and went to investigate.

Rune was standing at the kitchen sink in his low-slung jeans and sexy white T-shirt—both of them *very* fine ideas—with his hands thrust deep into the soapy water, scrubbing away.

"You don't have to do that," I said.

"I thought I'd start earning my keep," he said easily, then pulled a gleaming aluminum pan from the suds and held it up proudly.

All fine and well, except I didn't own a gleaming aluminum pan.

I did, however, own a somewhat pricy nonstick pan....

At least, I used to.

Rune said, "It took some elbow grease, but I finally got all the black off."

Wow.

People are always going on about how having an auxiliar will make your life easier. But my apartment was so decimated I thought I'd been the victim of a break-in, and my auxiliar sorely needed a rundown on the advent of Teflon. Maybe I should've tempered my expectations to avoid yet another case of buyer's remorse.

And yet, when Rune turned those pale jade eyes on me and flashed his secret smile, I felt no regret whatsoever. Only a welling sense of elation deep in my chest that made me feel as if I might float away like the soap bubbles that drifted out when Rune gave the bottle another long squeeze.

Boy, that was gonna take forever to rinse off.

"Hey, look, don't worry about cleaning up just now." I took the ruined pan from his soapy hands and set it in the drainer. "Listen to me, Rune. People might make auxiliars out to be glorified servants, but that's not how I see you." Given the state of the apartment, if what I'd been hoping for was a magical housekeeper, I'd be stunningly disappointed. "I don't care if I paid twenty dollars or twenty million dollars. You're not here to cater to my whims. You're your own person—you should do what makes you happy."

"I don't need to do things to *make* myself happy, Conrad. I already am." Rune's secret smile deepened. "But I can't tell you how tickled I am that you just referred to me as a person. All these extremities really are a lot to keep track of."

Maybe that was the big epiphany I'd take away from having an auxiliar—that mindset was what really counted. Since the goal is always moving, we might as well focus on enjoying the journey.

And maybe it didn't matter which tool I started training with...so long as I let myself begin.

When Rune attempted to rinse off his hands, a mass of soap suds volcanoed out of the sink and slopped to the floor. I wrested the sprayer from him, knocking the paprika off the spice rack in the process. The jar popped open and dusted everything red.

And that giddy feeling in my chest only grew lighter.

We spent the day putting the apartment back together. Rune might be good at controlling his appendages—ahem—but he nearly lost one of those appendages in the garbage disposal the minute I turned my back. And yet, his unfamiliarity with even the most basic things wasn't frustrating in the least. It only meant we needed to work together closely... and that was no great hardship at all.

Maybe I *had* managed to pick out the world's least helpful auxiliar. But there wasn't a doubt in my mind that I'd made the right decision.

———————————•●•———————————

Under my careful guidance, with only a few minor mishaps

(I didn't much care for that throw rug anyway) eventually, the apartment was wrangled into some kind of order. Yay, teamwork. I can't say the cleanup went any faster than it would have if I'd been by myself...but it was a heck of a lot more fun.

I was just wiping the last bits of dish soap from the kitchen cabinets when I heard Rune murmur, "Now, what have we here?"

He'd treated the air conditioner, the Roomba and the remote control with similar interest, so it wasn't the words themselves that I noticed.

It was the way in which he'd said them.

I slid out of the still-soapy kitchen just in time to find him opening Hester's toolbox.

"Be careful," I shouted as I flailed to keep my balance on the slick linoleum. "Those are really dangerous."

"I'm *well* aware." Rune plucked the Spintastic from its compartment and held it up for inspection. "I've seen a careless tinker nearly twist off his own head with one of these... though I suspect it wasn't the tool to blame, but the tipples he took from the flask in his pocket."

I'd spent all day explaining even the simplest of things to him, so I'd somehow managed to overlook the fact that he was literally old as dirt. And while he was baffled by wi-fi, he might know plenty about magichanicals.

Even so, I didn't venture any closer as he tossed the Spintastic in the air, flipped it upside down and squinted at some lettering on the handle. Probably the safety warning. "Cleveland, 1948. A fine vintage."

Figuring that all he would do was check the pedigree, I began to exhale...and nearly choked when Rune hit a button and a crazy articulated spring arm popped out. It was huge—way too big to have come from such a small handle—and it gave off a sound like a thin sheet of metal being flexed. "Too bad we don't have any stubborn valves or fittings lying around. I always got a kick out of these things."

"You're trained in a Spintastic?"

"Of course not." A quick gesture, and the spring folded itself neatly and clicked back into its housing. "No need to train the trainer—I was at Apex back when these were manufactured. Fun times."

He snapped the tool back into its compartment and pulled out the Through 'n Through. "Ah, now here's one that requires complete sobriety."

I slid back a step, bonking into the half-wall, but Rune was unperturbed. He spun a dial and flicked it on, then aimed it at a stack of junk mail in the recycling. Clicking it off, he plucked a grocery circular from the top, fanned it open, and peered at the minuscule hole he'd made. "Hm. This could stand to be recalibrated. I was aiming for one page but I got two instead."

"I had no idea it was capable of that much precision!"

Rune looked up from the junk mail and raised an eyebrow. "Then we'll need to fill your head with some fresh ideas."

It turned out my new auxiliar was not only well-versed in the safe operation of magichanical tools—he could practically make them sing. I watched in rapt fascination as he showed me how the Spintastic put a cordless screwdriver to shame and the Rejoinder could tack together something as fine as a single hair.

Unfortunately, despite my big epiphany to just start anywhere, seeing the tools put through their paces only made my impending decision more daunting. "How can I ever pick a tool to start training with when they all do such awesome things?"

Rune tilted his head in the way he did when I'd explained that people now paid money for bottled water. "Whatever do you mean? Just dig in and learn them all."

"I'm sure time is different for you—a dozen years must feel like practically nothing—but for me, it'll take a big chunk of time, proportionally speaking, to get the hang of any one of them."

As I spoke, he'd turned on his heel and swept down the hall while I followed, certain he didn't quite see that a decade was an awfully long time to a human like me. He dipped into the bedroom, and before I could wonder why, snatched Grandpa Joe's Apex clock off the wall. "Then it's a good thing you've got this."

"Be careful," I said breathlessly. "That's irreplaceable."

"Well, what do you know?" Rune tossed a dishtowel on the dining room table and placed the clock gently face-down. "Their plan worked after all."

"You lost me. Whose plan?"

"Apex management." He bent over the clock and blew off a bit of dust. "After the war, our assembly line was running like gangbusters. An Apex in every home, that was our goal. It was a point of great pride that we could spread magic far and wide, even to the poorest households, by combining it with mundane mechanics. But then we began finding that the more available the magichanicals were, the less people valued them. Pretty soon, our precious items were turning up in junkyards and swap meets. And we couldn't have that, now, could we?"

I thought of Magimart glutting the market with cheap knockoffs and devaluing the whole industry. "So you created scarcity to make people start to care again." I edged closer to the table and peered at the back of the clock. I'd never really looked at it from quite this angle, and now I realized that what I'd taken for a simple decorative plate was actually some sort of fitting, with only the finest of a hairline gap surrounding it.

"You should do the honors, Conrad." Rune pressed the Spintastic into my hand.

"But I don't know how."

He fit himself against my back—a lot more like a lover than a teacher—and enfolded my trembling hand in his. "Don't worry, I'll help. Just remember, this isn't only a tool. It's an idea."

I certainly had no lack of ideas—that was why it was so tough for me to choose among them. But with Rune guiding my hand, I was able to see what the next best step would be. I wasn't versed yet in the subtle gestures, but I was able to hold my goal in mind—my idea. And with only a few mishaps and a minor bout of dizziness, I was able to lift off the back panel of the clock.

I'd expected gears and cogs and machinery. But I hadn't expected it to look so organic, as if a miniature universe had somehow evolved inside the cavity of the clock, with the gears growing around each other and the cogs settling in together like they'd developed symbiotically.

Rune said, "It's been asleep for a while—but Apex magichanicals were made to work. It won't mind getting a wake-up call."

I followed the configuration of the various gears, from

obvious things like the dials, to less obvious things that I couldn't even begin to imagine the function...let alone which bit needed repair.

"It's the counterbalance," Rune said softly. "Sometimes precision parts like that get knocked out of alignment. Balance is a tricky thing. But all you'll need to do is snap it back into place." He glanced down at my phone on the corner of the table. "But you'd better hurry. It's almost midnight."

I didn't stop to ask why—and I didn't second-guess myself. The counterbalance was like a tiny barbell, and at the fulcrum where it normally rested, a tiny prong had broken off. The bit of metal was still there at the bottom of the casing. I tweezed it out, turned it around a few times to see how the break fit together, and reached for the Rejoinder.

But paused just short of picking it up.

Rune pressed his lips to my ear. "Remember, it's an idea. And if you have a hard time calling the idea of it whole and unbroken to mind, just look at the other prong and you'll figure it out."

I understood. It seemed way too simple to be true, but slippery, like I might forget the concept just as quickly as I'd grasped it. Before that could happen, I held the broken prong in place, picked up the Rejoinder, and flicked a button.

A button I hadn't even realized was there.

Like a magical welding torch, the Rejoinder let out a brilliant blue light. A curl of metallic smoke rose from the tiny part, but when I blinked away the spots that filled my vision, the part was in place again. "Good as new?" I asked.

"Stronger, probably. We took a lot of pride in our magichanicals—but we certainly weren't perfect." He took the Rejoinder from my hand and said, "Make sure you turn this off once your join is complete. If you accidentally seal off your airway, things could get ugly."

Right.

Once the Rejoinder was safely packed away, I placed the little barbell in its cradle, tipped the clock into an upright position, and watched.

Nothing happened...not until Rune reached past my shoulder and gave the counterweight a little tap. The barbell quivered. One end dipped down, the other up. And with a gentle click, it seesawed the other way.

As it settled into its motion, tiny gears caught, and the miniature universe inside sprang to life. It was like watching an old photograph burst into motion, unexpected and utterly enchanting. And as it found its rhythm, my simple little apartment filled with the soothing tick-tock of an active magichanical.

I blinked back a potentially embarrassing sentimental outburst, since it wouldn't do to cry into the clock's open cavity. I cleared my throat and said, "This clock has been broken ever since I can remember."

"Is that so?"

"It means the world to me to have it running again."

Rune replaced the back plate with an easy flick of the Spintastic. "Just wait till the magic begins."

I blinked, then realized I had no clue what he meant. "Wait—the what?"

Smiling his secret smile, Rune plucked the clock from my grasp, strode into the bedroom and remounted it on the wall.

It was 8:46 no more. The minute hand was now tracking through the numbers as quickly as a second hand, while the hour hand ticked along behind it. "Just give it a few moments to catch up," Rune said.

A self-setting clock? That would be handy when Daylight Savings Time started...or ended. Whichever thing it was that made me an hour late every spring. I checked my phone. Nearly midnight, which seemed poetic somehow. Then again, maybe that was just the romantic in me getting caught up in the joy of wielding the tools of my trade for the first time without losing an eye...or sealing it shut.

The hands whirred along until they reached 11:59, then paused—and trembled.

And then the whole face lit from within, and the numbers began to shift. Some digits rotated. Some flipped around. And others jiggled up and down like they could barely contain themselves. When all the hours finally sorted themselves out, a number 13 had appeared at the top of the circle.

"But I don't...understand." I turned to Rune for an explanation, and found he was surrounded by a gentle blue nimbus.

"The thirteenth hour," he said. "A pretty nifty function, making time stand still for an hour each day at midnight."

I considered this. "Only once a day? What about noon?"

"Just midnight."

"But the hour hand passes the twelve twice—"

"You're overthinking things again." Rune straightened the clock, which now read 13:01. "You can do an awful lot with seven extra hours a week."

Huh. "I always wondered why Grandpa Joe spoke four languages."

"Now we can tinker to your heart's delight. With your tools..." he caught my jeans by the belt loop and pulled me close. He nuzzled my hair, then added low and sultry, "Or with anything else that catches your eye."

The thirteenth hour would definitely take some getting used to. The utter silence surrounding us was a bit unnerving and the air felt syrupy-still. Yet I couldn't help but feel that every minute I'd wasted going back and forth, waffling about my choices and putting off major decisions, might now be recouped...with interest.

14

CONRAD

By the time Monday morning rolled around, I was confident enough to activate the Through 'n Through without wincing—or ripping myself a new butthole. But I wasn't so sure how Hester would react to this hot guy tagging along with me to work and claiming he was my auxiliar. I couldn't just leave him alone in the apartment, though. Not with nearly a third of a bottle of dishwashing liquid at his disposal.

And then there was Jeff. I texted him to go ahead without me. Oh, I'd introduce him to Rune at some point...but for now, I really couldn't bear the thought of him blathering on and on, all the way to work, about how awesome Magimart was and how the rest of us would soon be obsolete. I hated to think those mass-produced magichanical knockoffs were the wave of the future...but I worried that it just might be the case.

Rune and I took the long way to Three Corners—which essentially involved going around the same block twice—but we'd been in this bubble of fresh, new infatuation together all weekend and I didn't want it to end. Eventually, though we came to the end of the parking lot that took up the top third of the Y, and we paused and got our bearings.

"I'm glad you came back to Helping Hands after that daft auxiliar nearly impaled you," Rune said.

"I almost didn't, what with everyone trying to convince me an auxiliar was the last thing I needed." And the claws. Not gonna lie, they were pretty terrifying.

"But you didn't let that deter you."

"I felt a pull...and ignoring it wasn't an option."

"I knew you'd be back," Rune said simply. "Even when I wasn't quite awake, I could feel it—that certain something about your essence that makes you, you. When something is right—when someone is special—you just know."

We rounded the bus stop and spotted the Helping Hands storefront. Who was standing there in the doorway...but Jeff. And he was deep in conversation with the emo girl who'd "sold" me Rune. For twenty bucks.

"Conrad?" he called eagerly as I attempted to steer Rune across the street with a subtle nudge of my shoulder. "Hey, Conrad! Did you wanna weigh in on the whole Magimart scandal?"

I paused in my unsuccessful herding attempt, supposing it wasn't realistic to hope I'd get away without encountering Jeff and all his opinions that morning.

"Rune..." the woman said, drawing out the greeting so it was more of an innuendo. "You're awfully...awake."

"What can I say? It's a wakeful kind of day."

"You two know each other?" Jeff asked, then without waiting for answer, rambled on. "Talk about wakeful—people are waking up to the fact that Magimart isn't all it's cracked up to be. Dozens of complaints have been flooding the Chamber of Commerce. False advertising, unethical business practices, you name it. Magimart made a big splash here, all right—but not in the way they'd hoped."

Jeff must be in his glory, chatting up a cool girl who was willing to listen to him...more or less. Actually, she was mostly looking from Rune to me as if she could read all the X-rated things we'd done together this weekend like they were printed on our foreheads. And her eyes, I saw, were two entirely different colors—one blue, one a brown so pale it was nearly gold.

Talk about a fashion statement. No doubt Hester would have something to say about millennials and their contact lenses.

Jeff took in the nearby shops with a wave of his hand. "Maybe in other cities, where they don't have an awesome resource like Three Corners, people don't know any better. But around here, folks know a decent magical appliance when they see one. Magimart can't compete."

"But I thought you wanted to work there," I said to Jeff.

He not-so-subtly hauled me to one side and hissed, "This Helix chick is the new manager at Helping Hands—and she gave me her phone number! With no groveling whatsoever on my part! Only an idiot would want to work at Magimart when they could be right across the street from an awesome chick like *her*."

I guess there really is someone for everyone.

I left Jeff to his maladroit flirting and unlocked Arti-fix. The shop was cool and dim, smelling of old wood and funky magical agents, and the ambient whirring, humming tick-tock of magichanicals filled the air. Rune spun around, taking in all the old Apex products like a kid in a candy shop.

"Why, there's a Soup Cooler. And a Marble Hutch. And I'm hardly surprised to see the Bobbing Nobbin is on the fritz...I *told* them the spring bearing wouldn't hold up."

As he reacquainted himself with all the various magical machines, Hester's workroom door banged open and she peered out to see what all the conversation was about. Probably because it didn't sound like me getting chewed out by a customer, for once.

She narrowed her eyes at Rune, who was having a little chat with a nightlight that periodically flickered like a strobe lamp. But before she could ask who this strange man might be and why he was talking to her magichanicals, the metallic peacock strolled out behind her and startled us all with a very human-sounding scream.

Rune whirled around breathlessly. "Eureka? I wondered what had become of you."

"Rieer!"

"Well, I must say, the metallic feathers are delightful, especially with you wearing such a glorious tail as a peahen. I've always loved the way you march to the beat of your own drummer."

Hester opened her mouth to speak. Closed it again. Blinked, then said, "Well, I'll be damned. You picked out an auxiliar after all."

I cut my eyes to Rune, then turned back to Hester and said, "You can tell, even though he's a person?"

"Don't be dense—an auxiliar's form is only limited by its imagination." She looked Rune up and down, and told him, "I'm fine with you getting your hands dirty—heaven knows, Conrad could use the guidance—but don't go thinking you're on the payroll now."

Rune smiled. "Perish the thought."

"And don't start making Conrad's decisions for him, either. Best way for him to learn is to figure things out for himself."

"Rest assured," Rune said breezily. "I *have* done this a time or two."

Harrumphing under her breath, Hester ducked back into her workroom, followed by her grumbling peahen, and slammed the door.

I stared at the Do Not Disturb sign for a moment, then said to Rune, "You know Eureka?"

"You should have seen her as a Valkyrie. Glorious. And imposing enough to make a raiding band of marauders turn around and sail right back home."

Yeah...I could definitely picture it. "And all this time Hester's been so tough on me...it was for my own good?"

He prodded me playfully in the chest. "Turns out, you do have some discernment in there after all. Why else would you be so loyal to such a sourpuss?"

The workday went quickly with my new auxiliar there to keep me company. True to his word, Rune was no help at all in making decisions. But his upbeat mood was infectious, as well as his assurance that very few options were all good— or all bad. And while he might not be willing to relieve me of making any choices, when the crabby customer came back, he handled her so well that she not only didn't freak out about her phone charger, she bought a refurbished Apex Egg In-Shell Scrambler.

By the time we locked up, I'd handled a Rejoinder by

myself, plus I'd mended the delicate spindle on an Apex Spool Minder as well. And even Hester had nothing critical to say about it.

Normally, my best friend would be accosting me by now and telling me where I wanted to eat dinner. But tonight, Jeff was across the street at Helping Hands. I could see him through the shop window, talking at Helix with large, expressive gestures. Probably about mint condition Star Wars figures or saving throws.

Jeff's perfect girl. Though when she gave herself a quick stretch, her back arched in a way that wasn't quite human... and it occurred to me that the bald-headed clerk had said the *cat's* name was Helix. The cat with odd-colored eyes.

Had Jeff figured it out just yet? Somehow, I didn't think so—otherwise even he would be tongue-tied. Given how excited Jeff got when Captain Kirk managed to score with a female alien, he was in for a real treat.

As we watched their elaborate courting ritual like a pair of scientists doing animal research, something launched from the roof of the shop—a massive eagle with a wingspan wider than a Subaru. It gave a cry as it flew off into the darkening sky.

Rune waved to it heartily and called out, "Good job—you had us all fooled!" Then he turned to me and said, "Well, shall we go home and do a bit of tinkering?"

"Hester's spare tools are locked up in her workroom again."

The corner of his mouth lifted in that mesmerizing secret smile I could never possibly get enough of. He bent his head to mine, his botanical rosin scent teasing at my senses, and murmured, "Who said anything about tools?"

As the calls of the bald eagle grew distant, we walked back

to the apartment, talking about everything and nothing. I was still effervescing with the giddy feeling of new infatuation...and yet I also felt like I'd known Rune forever.

It just goes to show, when you meet the right one...your heart will be sure.

ABOUT THIS STORY

The last time I visited my dad, he'd bought an Alexa clock that could display both the time, and the countdown time on any timers he might have set. But calling the clock prone to breakdown would be an understatement. First, there was no glass covering over the hands, so you could physically move them. However, if you physically moved them, then they'd be out of synch with the smart workings, apparently forever. And there was no way to manually set them to the correct time—you had to go in through an app and have it synch to a device.

We finally made it read the correct time by telling the device it was in the middle of the Atlantic Ocean. And come Daylight Savings (beginning or end? Like Conrad I have no idea) it will be off by an hour.

But each time we tried a new time zone, the hands would quickly rotate around the face as if we were in a time-lapse. That's the mental image I had when Conrad and Rune got Grandpa Joe's clock working again, of the hands spinning around the dial to their own internal logic.

What would you do with an extra hour a day? I'd get more reading done, for sure.

There's a bald eagle that lives in Sheboygan. After I finished writing this story, I saw him myself for the first time, circling overhead as I was driving back from the swimming pool. It felt utterly magical.

If you enjoyed The Tinker's Apprentice, check out The ABCs of Spellcraft, a madcap, lighthearted series where paranormal cozy meets MM Romance, and the grumpy one loves the sunshine one.

If you're in the mood for a steamier, more dramatic paranormal read where the world's most awkward psychic medium faces off with all kinds of ghosts (ranging from quirky to scary), try the PsyCop series.

ABOUT THE AUTHOR

Jordan Castillo Price is usually pretty decisive, but would no doubt find the task of choosing an auxiliar fairly daunting... mainly because her cat is none too keen on sharing. She has a particular fondness for dusty old shops that smell like rosin.

Find more stories at www.jcpbooks.com

www.ingramcontent.com/pod-product-compliance
Lightning Source LLC
Chambersburg PA
CBHW061253170626
46809CB00007B/2971